THE
SNOW SPIDER

THE
SNOW SPIDER

Jenny Nimmo

Troll Associates

A TROLL BOOK, published by Troll Associates

Published by arrangement with Dutton Children's Books, a
division of Penguin Books USA Inc. For information address Dutton
Children's Books, a division of Penguin Books USA Inc.,
375 Hudson Street, New York, New York 10014.

First Troll Printing, 1991

Printed in the United States of America.

10 9 8 7 6 5 4 3 2

ISBN 0-8167-2264-1

for David

CONTENTS

THE FIVE GIFTS

Gwyn's grandmother gave him five gifts for his tenth birthday. They were very unusual gifts, and if Gwyn had not been the sort of boy he was, he might have been disappointed.

"Happy Birthday!" his grandmother said, turning her basket upside down.

Gwyn stared at the five objects that spilled out on the kitchen floor. A piece of seaweed, a yellow scarf, a tin whistle, a twisted metal brooch, and a small, broken horse. None of them was wrapped in bright birthday paper.

"Thank you, Nain!" said Gwyn, calling his grandmother by the name she liked best.

"Time to find out if you are a magician, Gwydion Gwyn!" said Nain.

"A magician?" Gwyn inquired.

"Time to remember your ancestors: Math, Lord of Gwynedd, Gwydion, and Gilfaethwy!"

"Who?"

"The magicians, boy! They lived here, in these mountains, maybe a thousand years ago, and they could do anything they wanted—turn men into eagles and soldiers into dust. They could make dreams come true. And so, perhaps, can you!"

On special occasions Nain often said peculiar things. Gwyn could not think of a reply.

"There has been an ache in this house since your sister . . . went," said Nain, "the ache of emptiness. You need help. If you have inherited the power of Gwydion, you can use it to get your heart's desire." She turned on her heel. "I won't stay for tea!"

"We've only just had breakfast, Nain!"

"Nevertheless . . ." She swept away, down the hallway and through the open front door, her black hair sparkling in the golden mist that hung over the garden, her dress as gaudy as the autumn flowers by the gate. Then she looked back and sang out, "Give them to the wind, Gwydion Gwyn, one by one, and you'll see!"

Gwyn took the gifts up to his bedroom and laid them on the windowsill. They seemed very unlikely props for a magician.

"What's she going on about now?" He scratched at his uncombed hair. From his tiny attic window he could see Nain's dark head bobbing down the mountain track. "She travels too fast for a grandmother,"

Gwyn muttered. "If my ancestors were magicians, does that make her a witch?"

His father's voice roared up the stairs, "Have you done the chickens, Gwyn? It's Saturday. What about the gate? The sheep will be in the garden again. Was that your grandmother? Why didn't she stay?"

Gwyn answered none of these questions. He gathered Nain's gifts together, put them in a drawer, and went downstairs. His father was outside, shouting at the cows as he drove them down the path to pasture.

Gwyn sighed and pulled on his boots. His grandmother had delayed him, but she had remembered his birthday. His father did not wish to remember. There was no rest on Saturday for Gwyn. No time for football matches, no bicycle ride to the town. He was the only help his father had on the farm, and weekends were days for catching up with all the work he had missed during the week.

Gwyn tried not to think of Bethan, his sister, as he scattered corn to the hens and searched for eggs in the barn. But when he went to examine the gate, he could not forget.

Beyond the vivid autumn daisies there was a cluster of white flowers nestling beneath the stone wall. Bethan had brought them up from the woods and planted them there, safe against the winds that tore across the mountain. Perhaps even then she had known that one day she would be gone, and had wanted to leave something for them to remember her by.

"Gwyn, I've something for you." His mother was leaning out of the kitchen window.

"I've got to do the gate, Dad says!"

"Do it later. It's your birthday, Gwyn. Come and see what I've got for you!"

Gwyn dropped his tool box and ran inside.

"I've only just wrapped it," his mother apologized. "Did Nain bring you anything?"

"Yes. I thought everyone else had forgotten."

"Of course not. I was so busy last night, I couldn't find the paper. Here you are!" His mother held out something very small, wrapped in shiny green paper.

Gwyn took the present, noticing that the paper had gold stars on it.

"I chose the paper specially." Mrs. Griffiths smiled anxiously.

"Wow!" Gwyn tore off the paper. Inside was a black watch in a transparent plastic box. Instead of numbers, tiny silver moons encircled its dark face. As Gwyn moved it, the hands sparkled like shooting stars.

"Oh, thanks, Mam!" He clasped the box to his chest and flung his free arm round his mother's neck.

"It's from us both, Gwyn. Your dad and me!"

"Yes, Mam," Gwyn said, though he knew his mother had not spoken the truth. His father did not give him gifts.

"I knew you'd like it. Always looking at the stars, you are, you funny boy. Take care of it now!"

." 'Course I will. It's more the sort of present for a magician. Nain gave me such strange things."

His mother drew away from him. "What things? What do you mean, a magician? Has Nain been spouting nonsense again?"

"Come and see!" Gwyn led his mother up to the attic and opened his top drawer. "There!" he pointed to Nain's gifts.

Mrs. Griffiths frowned at the five objects laid in a row on Gwyn's white school shirt. "Whatever is she up to now? I wish she wouldn't." She picked up the broken horse and turned it over in her hands.

"It has no ears," Gwyn remarked, "and no tail. Why did she give me a broken horse?"

"Goodness knows!" His mother held the horse closer and peered at a tiny label tied round its neck. "It's in Welsh," she said, "but it's not your grandmother's writing. It's so faint. *Dim hon,* I think that's what it says. 'Not this'!"

"What does it mean, Mam, *Not this*? Why did she give it to me if I'm not supposed to use it?"

His mother shook her head. "I never know why Nain does things."

"She said it was time to see if I was a magician like my ancestors."

"Don't pay too much attention to your grandmother," Mrs. Griffiths said wearily. "She's getting old and she dreams."

5

"Her hair is black," Gwyn reminded her.

"Her hair is black, but her eyes don't see things the way they used to!" Mam picked up the yellow scarf. "This too? Did Nain bring this?"

"Yes. It's Bethan's isn't it?"

His mother frowned. "It disappeared with her. She must have been wearing it the night she went, but the police found nothing the next morning, nothing at all. How strange! If Nain found it why didn't she say?" She held the scarf close to her face.

"You can smell the flowers," said Gwyn. "D'you remember? She used to dry the roses and put them in her clothes."

His mother laid the scarf back in the drawer. "Don't talk of Bethan now, Gwyn," she said.

"Why not, Mam? We should talk of her. It was on my birthday she left. She might come back . . . if we think of her."

"She won't come back! Don't you understand, Gwyn? We searched for days. The police searched— not only here, but everywhere. It was four years ago!" His mother turned away, then said more kindly, "I've asked Alun Lloyd to come up for tea. We'll have a proper celebration today, not like your other birthdays. You'd better get on with your work now."

When Mrs. Griffiths had left the room, Gwyn lifted the scarf out of the drawer and pressed it to his face. The scent of roses was still strong, and Bethan seemed very near. How good she had looked in her yellow scarf, with her dark hair and her red raincoat all bright and shining. He remembered now; she had been wearing the scarf that night, the night she had climbed the mountain and never come back. Why had Nain kept it secret all this time and only given it to him now, on his birthday?

"If Bethan left her scarf," Gwyn exclaimed aloud, "perhaps she meant to come back."

He laid the scarf over the broken horse, the seaweed, the whistle, and the brooch, and gently closed the drawer. He was humming cheerfully to himself when he went out into the garden again.

Mam kept her word. Alun Lloyd arrived at four o'clock, but he brought his twin brothers with him. That was not part of the arrangement.

There were nine Lloyds all crammed into a farmhouse only one room larger than the Griffiths'. Sometimes Mrs. Lloyd, ever eager to acquire a little more space, took it upon herself to send three or four children where only one had been invited. She was, however, prepared to pay for these few precious hours of peace. Alun, Gareth, and Siôn had all brought gifts. Mrs. Griffiths, guessing the outcome of her invitation, had provided tea for seven.

Kneeling on the kitchen floor, Gwyn tore the colored paper off his presents: a red kite, a pen, and a pair of black plastic spectacles with a large pink nose, black eyebrows, and a black moustache attached.

"Looks like your dad, doesn't it?" Siôn giggled, and he snatched up the spectacles, put them on, and began to prance up and down the room, chest out and fingers tucked behind imaginary suspenders.

Suddenly it was like other people's birthdays—the way a birthday should be, but Gwyn's never was.

Nain arrived with a box under her arm. "For your birthday," she said. "Records. I don't want them any more."

"But Nain, you've given your presents," said Gwyn.

"Don't look a gift horse in the mouth," Nain retorted. "Who are these nice little boys?"

"You know who they are. The Lloyds, Alun and Gareth and Siôn, from Tŷ Llŷr. Don't you ever see your neighbors?" chided Gwyn.

"Not the one with the specs. I don't know that one. Looks like your father." Nain chuckled. "Put on some music, Glenys!"

"Well, I don't know. . . ." Mrs. Griffiths looked worried. "Ivor put the record player away. We haven't used it since . . ."

"Time to get it out then," said Nain.

Somewhat reluctantly, Mrs. Griffiths knelt in the corner of the kitchen and withdrew the record player from a small neglected cupboard. She placed it on the kitchen table while the boys gathered round.

"I can't remember where to plug it in," said Mrs. Griffiths.

8

"The light, Mam," Gwyn explained. "Look, the plug is for the light."

"But . . . it's beginning to get dark." His mother sounded almost afraid.

"Candles! We can have candles!" Gwyn began to feel ridiculously elated. He fetched a box of candles from the cupboard and set them up on saucers and bottles all around the room.

Then they put on one of Nain's records. It was very gay and very loud: a fiddle, a flute, a harp, and a singer. The sort of music to make you dance wildly, and the Lloyds went wild. They drummed on the table, jumped on the chairs, stamped on the floor, waved the dish towels, juggled with the cat. The cat objected, and Siôn retired, temporarily, from the merrymaking, bloody-eared but unbowed.

In her purple dress and black lace stockings, Nain began to dance, her dark curls bouncing and her colored beads flying. She wore silver bracelets, too, which jangled when she raised her arms. Her black shawl swung out and made the candles flicker.

> *Mae gen i dipyn o dŷ bach twt*
> *A'r gwynt i'r drws bob bore.*
> *Hei di ho, di hei di hei di ho,*
> *A'r gwynt i'r drws bob bore . . .*

sang the singers, and so sang Nain in her high quivering voice.

The Lloyds thought it the funniest thing they had ever seen. Clutching their sides, they rolled on the floor, gasping and giggling.

Gwyn smiled, but he did not laugh. There was something strange, almost magical, about the tall figure spinning in the candlelight.

Down in the field, Gwyn's father heard the music. For a few moments he paused and listened while his cows, eager to be milked, ambled on up to the farmyard. Mr. Griffiths regarded the mountain rising dark and bare beside the house and remembered his daughter.

When the boys had breath left neither for dancing nor laughter, Mrs. Griffiths tucked the record player away in its corner, stood up, and removed her apron. Then she patted her hair, smoothed her dress, and said rather quiet and coy, "Tea will be in here today, boys!" She walked across the hallway and opened the door into the front room.

Gwyn was perplexed. Teas, even fairly fancy teas with relatives, were always in the kitchen these days. He moved uncertainly towards the open door and looked in.

A white cloth had been laid on the long oak table, so white it almost hurt his eyes. And upon the cloth, the best blue china, red napkins, plates piled with brightly wrapped candies, with sugar mice and chocolate pigs.

There were chips and popcorn, and cakes with colored icing on a silver stand. There were snappers too, decorated with gold and silver paper, and in the center of the table a magnificent sea of ice cream.

The Lloyds crowded into the doorway beside Gwyn and gazed at the splendid spread. Gwyn felt so proud. "Oh, Mam," he breathed. "Oh, Mam!"

Then Gareth and Siôn rushed past him and pulled out their chairs exclaiming, "Gwyn! Gwyn, come on, let's start, we're starving!"

"It's the grandest birthday table I've ever seen," said Alun. "Our Mam has never done anything like that."

"Nor has his, until today," said Nain. "It was about time."

Gwyn took his place at the head of the table and they began. There was so much chatter, so much laughter, no one heard Mr. Griffiths come in from milking and go upstairs. And Mrs. Griffiths, happy and gratified, did not notice her husband's boots beside the back door, nor his coat upon the hook, when she went into the kitchen to get the birthday cake.

The cake was huge and white, with chocolate windows and silver banners and on each of the ten towers, a flaming candle.

"Turn out the lights!" cried Gareth. He sprang to the switch, plunging the party into cosy candlelight.

"Blow out the candles, Gwyn, and wish!" commanded Siôn.

Gwyn drew a deep breath and then paused. "Let's

cut the cake and leave the candles," he said. "They look so good. Let's leave them till they die."

They were still lit when Mr. Griffiths came downstairs again. Snappers were snapping, and no one heard his feet upon the tiled kitchen floor, tapping in unfamiliar shoes. When the door opened, the tiny flames glowed fiercely for a moment and then died.

Except for a white shirt Mr. Griffiths was dressed entirely in black. He stared at the table in cold disbelief.

The shock of the electric light jolted the party out of its homey cheerfulness. The birthday table looked spoiled and untidy. Someone had spilled orange juice on the white cloth.

"What's this? Celebrating are we?" Mr. Griffiths' mouth was tight, his face white with displeasure.

Siôn was still wearing the spectacle mask, and his brothers began to giggle. He did resemble Mr. Griffiths.

"It's Gwyn's birthday, Ivor," Mrs. Griffiths explained nervously. "You're just in time for—"

"I know what day it is." Her husband spoke the words slowly through clenched teeth, as though the taste were bitter. "There are candles wasting in the kitchen, chairs on the floor, and look at this . . . litter!" He flung out his hand, indicating the table.

"Sit down, Ivor Griffiths, you miserable man," said Nain, "and celebrate your son's birthday!"

"Miserable is it?" Mr. Griffiths' big red hands were clasped tight across his chest, one hand painfully rubbing and pressing the other. "Miserable is it, to be remembering my own daughter who is gone? My daughter who went on this day, four years ago?"

Suddenly Mrs. Griffiths stood up. "Enough! We've had enough, Ivor!" she protested. "We remember Bethan too. We've mourned her going every year on this day, for four years. But it's Gwyn's birthday, and we've had enough of mourning! Enough! Enough!" She was almost crying.

Gwyn turned away. He did not want to look at the bright colors on the table, nor to see his friends' faces. He knew that his birthday was over. His mother was talking, but he could not listen to the words as she ushered his friends out. He heard them shuffling into the kitchen, murmuring good-bye, but he could not move. His father was still standing by the table, sad and silent in his black suit.

"How could you do that, Ivor?" Nain reproached her son as the front door slammed.

"How could I? I have done nothing. It was that one!" He looked at Gwyn. "She is gone because of him, my Bethan is."

It was said.

Gwyn felt almost relieved. He got up slowly and pushed his chair neatly back to the table. Without looking at his father, he walked out to the kitchen.

His mother was standing by the sink, waving to the Lloyds through a narrow window. She swung round quickly when she heard her son. "I'm sorry, Gwyn," she said quietly. "So sorry." She came towards him and hugged him close. Her face was flushed and she had put her apron on again.

"It was a great party, Mam! Thanks!" said Gwyn. "The other boys liked it too. I know they did."

"But I wanted your father to—"

"It doesn't matter, Mam," Gwyn interrupted quickly. "It was grand. I'll always remember it!"

He drew away from his mother and ran up to his room, where he sat on the edge of his bed, smiling at the memory of his party and the way it had been before his father had arrived. Gwyn knew his father could not help the bitterness that burst out of him every now and again, and he had developed a way of distancing himself from the ugly words: He thought hard about the good times, until the bad ceased to exist.

A tiny sound caused him to go to the window. There was a light in the garden, a lantern swaying in the evening breeze.

Gwyn opened the window. "Who's there?" he called.

He was answered by a high, girlish laugh, and then his grandmother's voice. "Remember your gifts, Gwydion Gwyn. Remember Math, Lord of Gwynedd. Remember Gwydion and Gilfaethwy!"

"Are you being funny, Nain?"

There was a long pause and then the reply, "It's not a game I'm playing, Gwydion Gwyn. Once in every seven generations the power returns—so they say.

Your father never had it, nor did mine. Let's find out who you are!"

The gate clicked shut and the lantern went swinging down the lane. The words of an old song rose and fell on the freshening wind until the light and the voice faded altogether.

Before he shut the window, Gwyn looked up at the mountain and remembered his sixth birthday. It had been a fine day. Like today. But in the middle of the night a storm had broken. The rain had come pouring down the mountainside in torrents, boulders and branches rumbling and groaning in its path. The Griffiths family had awakened, pulled the blankets closer to their heads, and fallen asleep again. Except for Gwyn. His black sheep was still up on the mountain. He had nursed it himself as a motherless lamb, wrapping it in Mam's old pullover, cosy by the fire. He had fed it with a bottle five times a day, until it had grown into a fine ewe.

"Please, get her! Please, save her!" Gwyn had shaken his sister awake.

Bethan had grumbled, but because she was older, and because she was kind, she had agreed to try to find his sheep.

The last time Gwyn saw her she had been standing by the back door in her red raincoat, testing the big outdoor flashlight. It was the night after Halloween, and the pumpkin was still on the windowsill, grimacing with its dark gaping mouth and sorrowful eyes.

Bethan had become strangely excited, as though she were going to meet someone very special, not just a lonely black ewe. "Shut the door tight when I am gone," she had whispered, "or the wind will howl through the house and wake Mam and Dad!" Then, swinging the yellow scarf round her dark hair, she had walked out into the storm. Bethan had never been afraid of anything.

Through the kitchen window, Gwyn had watched the beam of light flashing on the mountainside until it disappeared. Then he had fallen asleep on the rug beside the stove.

They never saw Bethan again, though they searched every inch of the mountain. They never found a trace of her perilous climb on that wild night, nor did they find the black ewe. The girl and the animal seemed to have vanished!

ARIANWEN

Unlike most Novembers, calm days seemed endless that autumn. Gwyn had to wait three weeks for a wind. It was the end of the month and the first snow had fallen on the mountain.

During those three weeks he found he dared not bring up the subject of his ancestors, though he dwelt constantly on Nain's words. Since his birthday, the atmosphere in the house had hardly been conducive to confidences. His father was remote and silent. His mother was in such a state of anxiety that whenever they were alone, he found he could only discuss the trivia of their days: the farm, the weather, his school activities.

But every morning and every evening Gwyn would open his drawer and take out the yellow scarf. He would stand by his window and run his hands lightly over the soft wool, all the time regarding the bare, snowcapped mountain, and he would think of Bethan.

Then one Sunday the wind came, so quietly at first that you hardly noticed it. By the time the midday roast had been consumed, however, twigs were flying, the barn door was banging, and the howling in the chimney was loud enough to drive the dog away from the stove.

Gwyn knew it was time.

"Who were my ancestors?" he asked his mother.

They were standing by the sink, Gwyn dutifully drying the dishes, his mother with her hands deep in the soapy water. "Ancestors," she said. "Well, no one special that I know of. . . ."

"No one?" he probed.

"Not on my side, love. Your grandfather's a baker, you know that. And before that, well . . . I don't know. Nothing special."

"What about Nain?"

Slouched in a chair by the stove, Gwyn's father rustled his newspaper but did not look up.

Gwyn screwed up his courage. "What about your ancestors, Dad?"

Mr. Griffiths peered, unsmiling, over his paper. "What about them?"

"Anyone special? Nain said there were magicians in the family . . . I think."

His father shook the newspaper violently. "Nain has

some crazy ideas," he said. "I had enough of them when I was a boy."

"Made you try and bring a dead bird back to life, you said," his wife reminded him.

"How?" asked Gwyn.

"Chanting!" grunted Mr. Griffiths. It was obvious that, just as Nain had said, his father had not inherited whatever strange power it was those long-ago magicians had possessed. Or if he had, he did not like the notion.

"They're in the old legends," mused Mrs. Griffiths, "the magicians. One of them made a ship out of seaweed, Gwydion I think it—"

"Seaweed?" Gwyn broke in.

"I think it was and—"

"Gwydion?" Gwyn absentmindedly pushed his wet dish towel into an open drawer. "That's my name?"

"Watch what you're doing, Gwyn," his mother complained. "You haven't finished."

"Math, Lord of Gwynedd, Gwydion, and Gilfaethwy. And it was Gwydion that made the ship? Me . . . my name!"

"It's what you were christened—Nain wanted it. But"—Mrs. Griffiths glanced in her husband's direction—"your father never liked it, not when he remembered where it came from. So we called you Gwyn. Dad was pretty fed up with all of Nain's stories."

Mr. Griffiths dropped his newspaper. "Get on with

your work, Gwyn," he ordered, "and stop upsetting your mother."

"I'm not upset, love."

"Don't argue and don't defend the boy!"

They finished the dishes in silence. Then, with the wind and his ancestors filling his thoughts, Gwyn rushed upstairs and opened the drawer. But he did not remove the seaweed. The first thing he noticed was the brooch, lying on top of the scarf. He could not remember having replaced it that way. Surely the scarf was the last thing he had returned to the drawer.

The sunlight slanting through his narrow window fell directly on the brooch, and its contorted shapes slowly assumed the form of a star, then a snowflake. A group of petals changed into a creature with glittering eyes and then became a twisted piece of metal again. Something or somebody wanted him to use the brooch!

Gwyn picked it up and thrust it into his pocket. Grabbing his coat from a chair he rushed downstairs and out the back door. As he raced across the yard, he heard a voice calling him to a chore. "But the wind was too loud, wasn't it?" he shouted joyfully to the sky. "I never heard nothing!"

He banged the yard gate to emphasize his words and began to run through the field. After a hundred yards the land began to rise. He kept to the sheeptrack for a while, then climbed a wall and jumped down into another field, this one steep and bare. He was among the sheep now, scattering them as he bounded over mounds and boulders. Stopping at the next wall, he took a deep breath. The mountain had begun in earnest. Now it had to be walking or climbing; running was impossible.

A sense of urgency gripped him, an overwhelming feeling that today, perhaps within that very hour, something momentous would occur.

He stumbled on, now upon a sheeptrack, now heaving himself over boulders. He had climbed the mountain often, sometimes with Alun, sometimes alone, but the first time had been with Bethan, one summer long ago. It had seemed an impossible task then, when he was not even five years old, but she had willed him to the top, comforting and cajoling him with her gentle voice. "It's so beautiful when you get there, Gwyn. You can see the whole world . . . well, the whole of Wales anyway. And the sea and clouds below you. You won't fall; I won't let you!" She had been wearing the yellow scarf that day. Gwyn remembered how it had streamed out across his head, like a banner, when they reached the top.

It was not a high mountain nor a dangerous one. Some might even call it a hill. It was wide and grassy, a series of gentle slopes that rose, one after another, patterned with stone walls and windblown bushes. The plateau at the top was a lonely place, however. From here only the empty fields and surrounding mountains could be seen, and, far out to the west, the distant gray line of the sea. Gwyn took shelter beside the tallest rock, for the wind sweeping across the plateau threatened to roll him back down.

He surely must have found the place to offer his brooch. "Give it to the wind," Nain had said. Bracing himself against the rock, Gwyn extended his upturned hand into the wind and uncurled his fingers.

The brooch was snatched away so fast that he never saw what became of it. He withdrew his hand and waited for the wind to answer, not knowing what the answer would be, but wanting it to bring him something that would change the way things were, to fill the emptiness in the house below.

But the wind did not reply. It howled about Gwyn's head and tore at his clothes. Then slowly it died away, taking the precious brooch somewhere within its swirling streams and currents and leaving nothing in return.

Then, from the west, came a silver white cloud of snow, obscuring the sea, the surrounding mountains, and the fields below. And, as the snow began to encircle and embrace him, Gwyn found himself chanting, "Math, Lord of Gwynedd, Gwydion, and Gilfaethwy!" This he repeated over and over again, not knowing whether he was calling to the living or the dead. And all the while huge snowflakes drifted silently about him, melting as they touched him, so that he did not turn into the snowman that he might otherwise have become.

Gwyn stood motionless for what seemed like hours, enveloped in a soft, serene whiteness, waiting for an answer. Yet had Nain promised him an answer? In the stillness he thought he heard a sound, very high and light, like icicles on glass.

His legs began to ache. His face grew numb with cold, and when night clouds darkened the sky, he began his descent, resentful and forlorn.

The lower slopes of the mountain were still green. The snow had not touched them, and it was difficult for Gwyn to believe he had been standing deep in snow just minutes earlier. Only from the last field could the summit be seen, but by the time Gwyn reached the field, the mountain was hidden by mist. He could not tell if snow still lay above.

It was dark when he got home. Before opening the back door he stamped his boots. His absence from the farm all day would not be appreciated, he knew. He did not wish to aggravate the situation with muddy boots. He raised his hand to brush his shoulders free of the dust he usually managed to collect, and his fingers encountered something icy cold.

Believing it to be a snowflake or even an icicle, Gwyn plucked it off his shoulder and moved closer to the kitchen window to examine what he had found. His mother had not yet drawn the curtains, and light streamed into the yard.

It was a snowflake, the most beautiful he had ever seen, for it was magnified into an exquisite and intricate pattern: a star glistening like crystal in the soft light. And then the most extraordinary thing happened. The star began to move, and Gwyn stared amazed as it gradually assumed the shape of a tiny silver spider. Had the wind heard him after all? Was he a magician then?

"Gwyn, is that you out there? You'll have no tea if you hang about any longer." His mother had spied him from the window.

Gwyn closed his fingers over the spider and tried to open the back door with his left hand. The door was jerked back violently and his father pulled him into the kitchen.

"What the hell are you doing out there? You're late! Can't you open a door now?" Mr. Griffiths had flecks of mud on his spectacles. Gwyn tried not to look at them.

"My hands are cold," he said.

"Tea'll be cold too," grumbled Mr. Griffiths. "Get your boots off and sit down. Where were you this afternoon? You were needed. That mad rooster's out again. We won't have a Christmas dinner if he doesn't stay put."

With some difficulty Gwyn managed to remove his boots with his left hand. "I'm just going upstairs," he said airily.

"Gwyn, whatever are you up to?" asked his mother. "Wash your hands and sit down."

"I've got to go upstairs," Gwyn insisted.

"But Gwyn . . ."

"Please, Mam!"

Mrs. Griffiths shrugged and turned back to the stove.

24

Her husband had begun to chew bacon and was not interested in Gwyn's hasty flight through the kitchen.

Rushing into his bedroom Gwyn scanned the place for something in which to hide his spider. He could think of nothing but the drawer. Placing the spider gently on the yellow scarf, he pushed the drawer back, leaving it open a few centimeters for air, then fled downstairs.

He got an interrogation in the kitchen.

Mrs. Griffiths began it. "Whatever made you run off like that this afternoon?" she complained. "Didn't you hear me call?"

"No, it was windy," Gwyn replied cheerfully.

"Well, what was it you were doing all that time? I rang Mrs. Lloyd. You weren't there."

"No," said Gwyn, "I wasn't!"

"Not giving much away, are you?" Mr. Griffiths muttered from behind a mug of tea. "It's no use trying to get that rooster now that it's dark," he went on irritably. "We'll have to be up early in the morning."

"Won't have any trouble waking if he's out," Gwyn sniggered.

"It would take more than a rooster to wake you some mornings," laughed his mother. At least she had recovered her good humor.

After tea Mr. Griffiths vanished into his workshop. His workload of farm repairs seemed to increase rather than diminish, and Gwyn often wondered if it was his father's way of avoiding conversation.

While his mother chattered about Christmas and the rooster, he thought impatiently of the drawer in his room. Excusing himself with a quick hug, Gwyn left his mother to talk to the cat and, trying not to show an unnatural enthusiasm for bed, crossed the hallway and climbed the stairs two at a time.

His bedroom door was open, and there appeared to be a soft glow within. On entering the room Gwyn froze. There were shadows on the wall: seven helmeted figures, motionless beside his bed. He turned, fearfully, to locate the source of light. It came from behind a row of toy spacemen standing on the chest of drawers. Gwyn breathed a sigh of relief and approached the spacemen.

The silver spider had climbed out of the drawer. It was glowing in the dark!

Gwyn brushed his toys aside and hesitantly held out his hand to the spider. It crawled into his open palm, and he gently raised it closer to his face. The spider's touch was icy cold, and yet the glow that it shed on Gwyn's face had a certain strange warmth that seemed to penetrate every part of his body.

He held the spider for several minutes, admiring the exquisite pattern on its back and wondering whether there was more to the tiny creature than a superficial beauty. It had come in exchange for the brooch, of that he was certain. But was it really he who had transformed the brooch? Or had the extraordinary spider come from a place beyond his world? He resolved to keep it a secret until he could consult his grandmother the following evening.

Replacing the spider in the drawer, Gwyn went downstairs to fetch a book. When he returned, the glow came from the bedpost. Deciding that he had no need of an electric light, Gwyn sat on the bed and read his book beside the spider. It was an exceptional sensation, reading by spiderlight.

Nain was gardening by lamplight when Gwyn came by her cottage. She was wearing her sunhat and a bright purple sweater. The sky was dark. Frost had begun to sparkle on the ground.

"It's a bit late for gardening, isn't it?" said Gwyn, approaching his grandmother down the gravel path.

"I like to poke a few things about," she replied, "just to let them know I've got my eye on them."

"There's not much growing, Nain," Gwyn remarked. "Not that you can see anything in this light."

"There's potatoes!" she said defiantly, pulling a plant out of the ground, scattering earth all over Gwyn's white shoes. Not satisfied with this, she shook the plant violently and Gwyn sprang back, too late to save the bottoms of his new school trousers.

"Oh, heck, Nain!" he cried. "What did you do that for? Now I'll get it."

"Why didn't you put your boots on, silly boy?" she replied. "There's mud all down the lane."

"I came for a chat. How was I to know I'd be attacked by a madwoman."

"Ha! Ha! Who's mad, Gwydion Gwyn?" Nain loved being teased. "Have you brought good news. Are you a magician, then?"

"Can't we go inside, Nain?" Gwyn fingered the matchbox in his pocket. He did not want to talk about the spider under the stars. Out here in the dark someone could be listening.

"Come on, then! We'll leave the plants to doze for a bit and have a cup of tea." Nain dropped her potatoes, shook out her sweater, and stamped across the ground to open the back door.

The inside of her house was like a bright bowl. All the corners had been rounded off with cupboards and bookcases, and upon every item of furniture was heaped a jumble of books, cheerful-colored clothes, and exotic plants. The fronds of shawls, trailing leaves, and garlands of beads festooned the furniture to such a degree that its identity could not easily be ascertained. The only source of light came from an oil lamp. As this was partially obscured by a tall fern, the whole place had a wild and mystical air about it.

Somewhere through the jungle a kettle lurked, and soon this was whistling merrily, while Nain sang from behind a screen embroidered with butterflies, and a canary chattered in its cage.

Gwyn looked around for a vacant seat. There was none. "What shall I do with the eggs, Nain?" he called.

"How many?"

Gwyn counted the eggs nestling in a red woolly hat on the armchair. "Seven," he replied.

"Well! Well! They've all been in here today, then, and I never noticed." Nain chuckled to herself.

"Why d'you let the hens in, Nain?" Gwyn asked. "They're such mucky things. Mam would have a fit."

"Huh! Your mam would have a fit if she looked under my bed, I expect." Nain giggled. "But there's no need to go upsetting people for nothing. Bring the eggs out here."

Gwyn held out the bottom of his sweater and gathered the eggs into it. He looked for his grandmother behind the screen, but she had vanished, and so had the kitchen. There was only a narrow space between rows of plants and meters of red velvet. He found the kettle on the windowsill and put the eggs in a green hat beside it. Nain did not seem to be short of hats, so he felt the eggs would be safe enough for the moment. However, she had been known to wear two at a time and so he called out, "Don't put your green hat on yet, Nain!"

His grandmother's head popped out from a gap in the velvet, "Isn't it grand?" she purred. "I'm going to dance in it."

"The hat?" Gwyn inquired.

"This, silly boy." His grandmother stroked the velvet material.

"Where?" he asked.

"Who knows?"

"Nain, would you find yourself a cup of tea and then sit down and—concentrate. I've got something to show you!" Gwyn fingered his matchbox again.

"Was it the wind?" Nain asked. "It was windy yesterday. I thought of you. Quick, a cup of tea." She withdrew her head and reappeared a moment later, carrying two blue enamel mugs. "One for you?"

"No thanks, Nain!" His grandmother did not use ordinary tea leaves. Her tea was made from nettles or dried roots. Sometimes it was palatable, but most often it was not. Today Gwyn preferred not to risk it.

He waited until his grandmother had settled herself in the armchair and sipped her tea before he knelt beside her and took out the matchbox. He wanted her undivided attention for his revelation. Even so, he was unprepared for the ecstatic gasp that accompanied Nain's first glimpse of the spider, as he gently withdrew the lid. The tiny creature crawled onto his hand, glowing in the dark room. Nain's eyes sparkled like a child's.

"How did it come?" Her whisper was harsh with excitement.

"In the snow," Gwyn replied. "I thought it was a snowflake. It was the brooch, I think. I gave it to the wind, like you said, and this . . . came back!"

"So," Nain murmured triumphantly, "you *are* a magician then, Gwydion Gwyn, as I thought. See what you have made!"

30

"But did I make it, Nain? I believe it has come from somewhere else. Some far, far place . . . I don't know, beyond the world, I think."

"Then you called it, you brought it here, Gwydion Gwyn. Did you call?"

"I did, but . . ." Gwyn hesitated. "I called the names you said into the snow: Math, Lord of Gwynedd, Gwydion, and Gilfaethwy. Those were the only words."

"They were the right words, boy. You called to your ancestors. The magicians heard your voice and took the brooch to where it had to go, and now you have the spider!" Nain took the spider from Gwyn and placed it on her arm. Then she got up and began to dance through the shadowy wilderness of her room. The tiny glowing creature moved slowly up her purple sleeve until it came to her shoulder. There it rested, shining like a star beneath her wild black curls.

Gwyn watched and felt that it was Nain who was the magician and he the enchanted one.

Suddenly his grandmother swooped back, took the spider from her hair, and put it gently into his hands. "Arianwen," she said. "White silver! Call her Arianwen. She must have a name!"

"And what now?" asked Gwyn. "What becomes of Arianwen? Should I tell about her? Take her to a museum?"

"Never! Never! Never!" said Nain fiercely. "They wouldn't understand. She has come from another world to bring you closer to the thing you want."

"I want to see my sister," said Gwyn. "I want things the way they were before she went."

Nain looked at Gwyn through half-closed eyes. "It's just the beginning, Gwydion Gwyn, you'll see. You'll be alone, mind. You cannot tell anyone. A magician can have his heart's desire if he truly wishes it, but he will always be alone." She propelled her grandson gently but firmly towards the door. "Go home now or they'll come looking. And *never tell a soul!*"

3

THE
GIRL IN THE WEB

The farmhouse was empty when Gwyn reached home. Mr. Griffiths could be heard drilling in his workshop. Mrs. Griffiths had popped out to see a neighbor, leaving a note for her son on the kitchen table,

Soup on the stove.
Heat it up if it's cold

"The soup or the stove?" Gwyn muttered to himself. He opened the stove door, but the red embers looked so warm and comforting he was reluctant to cover them with fresh coal. He turned off the light and knelt beside the fire, holding out his hands to the warmth.

He must have put the matchbox down somewhere, and he must have left it open, because he suddenly became aware that Arianwen was climbing up the back of the armchair. When she reached the top she swung down to the arm, leaving a silver thread behind her. Up she went to the top again, and then down, her silk glistening in the firelight. Now the spider was swinging and spinning back and forth across the chair so fast that Gwyn could only see a spark shooting over an ever-widening sheet of silver.

"A cobweb!" he breathed.

And yet it was not a cobweb. There was someone there. Someone was sitting where the cobweb should have been. A girl with long pale hair and smiling eyes: Bethan, sitting just as she used to sit, with her legs tucked under her and one hand resting on the arm of the chair, the other supporting her chin as she gazed into the fire. Still Arianwen spun, tracing the girl's face, her fingers, her hair, until every feature became so clear Gwyn felt he could have touched the girl.

The tiny spider entwined the silk on one last corner and then ceased her feverish activity. She waited, just above the girl's head, allowing Gwyn to contemplate her creation without interruption.

Was the girl an illusion? An image on a silver screen? No, she was more than that. Gwyn could see the impression her elbow made on the arm of the chair. He could see the fibers in her skirt and the lines on her slim, pale hand.

Only Bethan had ever sat like that. Only Bethan had gazed into the fire in just that way. But his sister was dark with rosy cheeks, her skin tanned golden by the wind. This girl was fragile and so silver-pale she might have been made of gossamer.

"Bethan?" Gwyn whispered. He stretched out his hand towards the girl.

A ripple spread across the shining image, as water moves when a stone hits it. Gwyn did not notice a cool draft entering the kitchen as the door began to open.

"Bethan?" he said again.

The figure shivered violently as the door swung wider and the light went on. The girl in the cobweb hovered momentarily, then began to fragment and fade until Gwyn was left staring into an empty chair. His hand dropped to his side.

"Gwyn! What are you doing, love? What are you staring at?" His mother came round the chair and looked down at him, frowning anxiously.

Gwyn found that speech was not within his power. Part of his strength seemed to have evaporated with the girl.

"Who were you talking to? Why were you sitting in the dark?" Concern caused Mrs. Griffiths to speak sharply.

Her son swallowed but failed to utter a sound. He stared up at her helplessly.

"Stop it, Gwyn! Stop looking at me like that! Get up! Say something!" His mother shook his shoulders and pulled him to his feet.

He stumbled over to the table and sat down, trying

desperately to drag himself away from the image in the cobweb. The girl had smiled at him before she vanished, and he knew that she was real.

Mrs. Griffiths ignored him now, busying herself about the stove, shovelling in coal, warming up the soup. By the time the soup sat steaming in a bowl before him, he had recovered enough to say, "Thanks, Mam!"

"Perhaps you can tell me what you were doing?" his mother persisted, calmer now that she had done something practical.

"I was just cold, Mam. It's nice by the stove when the door is open. I sort of . . . dozed and . . . couldn't wake up." Gwyn tried to explain away something his mother would neither believe nor understand.

"Well, you're a funny one. I would have been here, but I wanted to pickle some of those tomatoes, so I had to run down to Betty Lloyd for sugar." Mrs. Griffiths chattered on, somewhat nervously Gwyn thought, while he sat passively, trying to make appropriate remarks during her pauses.

His father's return from the workshop brought Gwyn to life. "Don't sit down, Dad!" he cried, leaping towards the armchair.

"What on earth? What's got into you, boy?" Mr. Griffiths was taken by surprise.

"It's a matchbox," Gwyn explained. "In the chair. I don't want it squashed."

"What's so special about a matchbox?"

"There's something in it, a particular sort of insect," stammered Gwyn. "For school," he added. "It's important, see?"

His father shook the cushions irritably. "Nothing there," he said, and sat down heavily in the chair.

"Here's a matchbox," said Mrs. Griffiths, "on the floor." She opened the box. "But there's nothing in it."

"Oh, heck!" Gwyn moaned.

"What sort of insect was it, love? Perhaps we can find it for you." His mother was always eager to help where school was concerned.

"A spider," Gwyn said.

"Oh, Gwyn," moaned Mrs. Griffiths, "not spiders. I've just cleaned this house from top to bottom. I can't abide cobwebs."

"Spiders eat flies," Gwyn retorted.

"There are no flies in this house," thundered Mr. Griffiths, "and when you've found your 'particular' spider, you keep it in that box. If I find it anywhere near my dinner, I'll squash it with my fist, school or no school!"

"You're a mean old . . . man!" cried Gwyn.

Mrs. Griffiths gave an anguished sigh as her husband stood up. But Gwyn fled before another word could be spoken. He climbed up to his bedroom. Nothing followed, not even a shout.

He turned on the light as soon as he entered the room, so he was not immediately aware of the glow coming from the open top drawer. As he walked over to the window to draw the curtains, he looked down and saw Arianwen sitting on the whistle. Incredibly, she must have pulled the whistle from beneath the yellow scarf. But as Gwyn considered this, he realized it was no doubt a small feat for a creature who had just conjured a girl in her web. And what about the girl? Had she been mere gossamer after all, a trick of the firelight on a silver cobweb?

"Why couldn't you stay where you were?" Gwyn inquired of the spider. "You caused me a bit of bother just now!"

Arianwen moved slowly to the end of the whistle. It occurred to Gwyn that she had selected it for some special purpose.

"Now?" he asked in a whisper.

Arianwen crawled off the whistle.

Gwyn picked it up and held it to his lips. It was cracked; only a thin sound came from it. He shrugged and opened the window. Arianwen climbed out of the drawer and swung herself onto his sleeve.

"But there's no wind," he said softly. He held his arm up to the open window. "See, no wind at all."

The spider crawled onto the window frame and climbed up to the top. When she reached the center she let herself drop on a shining thread until she hung just above Gwyn's head, a tiny lantern glowing against the black sky.

Gwyn had been wrong. There was a wind, for now

the spider was swaying in the open window. He could feel a breath of ice-cold air on his face.

"Shall I say something?" he mused. "What shall I say?"

Then, without any hesitation he called, "Gwydion! Gwydion! I am Gwydion! I am Math and Gilfaethwy!"

Even as he said the words, the breeze became an icy blast, rattling the window and tugging at his hair. He stepped back, amazed by the sudden violence in the air.

Arianwen spun crazily on her silver thread. The wind swooped into the room, tearing the whistle from Gwyn's hand and whisking it out through the open window.

Something shot into the bedroom and dropped with a crack onto the bare floorboards. It was a pipe of some sort, slim and silver like a snake. Gwyn stared at it apprehensively, then he slowly bent and picked it up. It was silky smooth and had an almost living radiance about it, as though it had no need of human hands to shine and polish it. Tiny, delicate lines encircled it, forming a beautiful pattern of knots and spirals. He had seen such a design on a gravestone somewhere, or framing the pictures in one of Nain's old books.

Almost fearfully, he put the pipe to his lips. But he did not play it. He felt that it had not come for that purpose. He sat on the bed and ran his fingers over the delicate pattern.

The window stopped rattling and the wind dropped to a whisper. The land was quiet and still again. Arianwen left her post and ran into the drawer.

Gwyn laid the pipe on his bedside table and shut the window. He decided that he was too tired to speculate on the evening's events until he was lying down. He turned off the light, undressed, and got into bed.

But he had awakened something that would not sleep, and now he was to be allowed no rest.

For a few moments Gwyn closed his eyes. When he opened them he saw that Arianwen had spun hundreds of tiny threads across the wall opposite his bed. They were so fine, so close, that they resembled a vast screen. Still she spun, swinging faster and faster across the wall, climbing, falling, weaving, not one thread at a time but a multitude. Soon the entire wall was covered, but the spider was not satisfied. She began to thread her way along the wall beside Gwyn's bed, over the door, over the cupboard, until the furniture was entirely covered with her irresistible flow of silk.

Gwyn was not watching Arianwen now. Something was happening in the web. He had the sensation that he was being drawn into it, deeper and deeper, faster and faster. He was plunging into black silent space. A myriad of tiny colored fragments burst and scattered in front of him, and then there was nothing. After a while the moving sensation began to slow until he felt that he was suspended in the air above an extraordinary scene.

A city was rising through clouds of iridescent snow.

First a tower, tall and white, surmounted by a belfry of finely carved ice. Within the belfry hung a gleaming silver bell. Beneath the tower there were houses, all of them white, all of them round and beautiful, with shining domelike roofs and oval windows latticed with delicate networks of silver—like cobwebs.

Beyond the houses there lay a vast expanse of snow, and surrounding the snow, mountains, brilliant under the sun—or was it the moon hanging there, a huge sphere glowing in the dark sky?

Until that moment the city had been silent. Suddenly the bell in the white tower began to sway and then it rang. Gwyn could hear it, clear and sweet over the snow. Children emerged from the houses, children with pale faces and silvery hair, chattering, laughing, singing. They were in the snowfields now, calling to each other in high melodious voices. Was this where the pale girl in the web had come from?

Suddenly another voice called. His mother was climbing the stairs. "Is that you, Gwyn? Are you awake? Was that a bell I heard?"

The white world shivered and began to fade until only the voices were left, singing softly in the dark.

The door handle rattled and Mrs. Griffiths stood in the doorway, silhouetted against the landing light. She was trying to tear something out of her hair. Finally she turned on the light and gave a gasp. "Ugh! It's a cobweb," she exclaimed, "a filthy cobweb!" For her the silky threads did not glitter. They appeared merely as a dusty nuisance. "Gwyn, how many spiders have you got up here?"

"Only one, Mam," he replied.

"I can hear singing. Have you got your radio on? It's so late."

"I haven't got the radio on, Mam."

"What is it then?"

"I don't know, Mam." Gwyn was now as bewildered as his mother.

The sound seemed to be coming from beside him. But there was nothing there, only the pipe. The city, the children, even the vast cobwebs were gone.

Gwyn picked up the pipe and put it to his ear. The voices were there, inside the pipe. He almost dropped it in his astonishment. So they had sent him a pipe to hear the things that he saw, maybe millions of miles away. The sound grew softer and was gone.

"Whatever's that? Where did you get it?" asked Mrs. Griffiths, approaching the bed.

Gwyn decided to keep the voices to himself. "It's a pipe, Mam. Nain gave it to me."

"Oh! That's all," she said, dismissing the pipe as though it was a trivial bit of tin. "Try and get some sleep now, love, or you'll never be up for the bus." She bent and kissed him.

"I'll be up, Mam," Gwyn assured her.

His mother went to the door and turned out the light. "That singing must have come from the Lloyds. They're always late to bed," she muttered as she went downstairs. "It's the cold. Funny how sound travels when it's cold."

Gwyn slept deeply but woke soon after dawn and felt for the pipe under his pillow. He took it out and listened. The pipe was silent. It did not even look as bright, as magical, as it had in the night. He was not disappointed. A magician cannot always be at work.

He dressed and went downstairs before his parents were awake. He had eaten his breakfast and fed the chickens by the time his father came downstairs to put the kettle on.

"What's got into you, then?" Mr. Griffiths inquired as Gwyn sprang through the kitchen door.

"Just woke up early. It's a grand day, Dad!" Gwyn said.

This statement received no reply, nor was one expected. The silences that sometimes opened between father and son created an unbearable emptiness that neither seemed able to overcome. But they had become accustomed to the situation, and if they could not entirely avoid it, they accepted it as best they could. It was usually Gwyn who fled from his father's company, but on this occasion he was preoccupied, and it was his father who left to milk the cows.

A few moments later Mrs. Griffiths shuffled down the stairs in torn slippers, still tying her apron strings. "Why didn't someone call me," she complained, irritated to find herself the last one down.

"It's not late, Mam," Gwyn reassured her, "and I've had my breakfast."

His mother began to bang and clatter about the kitchen. Gwyn retreated from the noise and went into the garden.

The sun was full up now. He could feel the warmth of it on his face. The last leaves had fallen during the wild wind of the night before, decorating the garden with splashes of red and gold. A mist hung in the valley, even obscuring his grandmother's cottage. Gwyn was glad that he lived in high country, where the air and the sky always seemed brighter.

At eight o'clock he began to walk down towards the main road. The school bus stopped at the end of the lane at twenty minutes past eight and did not wait for stragglers. It took Gwyn all of twenty minutes to reach the bus stop. For half a mile the route he took was little more than a steep path, rutted by the giant wheels of his father's tractor and the hooves of sheep and cattle. He had to leap over puddles, mounds of mud, and fallen leaves. Only when he had passed his grandmother's cottage did the path level off a little. The bends were less sharp, and something resembling a lane began to emerge. By the time it had reached the Lloyds' farmhouse, the lane had become a respectable size, paved and wide enough for two passing cars.

The Lloyds erupted through their gate, all seven of them, arguing, chattering, and swinging their bags.

44

Mrs. Lloyd stood behind the gate while little Iolo clasped her skirt through the bars, weeping bitterly.

"Stop it, Iolo. Be a good boy. Nerys, take his hand," Mrs. Lloyd implored her oldest child.

"Mam! Mam! Mam!" wailed Iolo, kicking his sister away.

"Mam can't come, don't be silly, Iolo! Alun, help Nerys. Hold his other hand."

Alun obeyed. Avoiding the vicious thrusts of his youngest brother's boot, he seized Iolo's hand and swung him off his feet. Then he began to run down the lane, the little boy still clinging to his neck and shrieking like a demon. The other Lloyds, thinking this great sport for the morning, followed close behind, whooping and yelling.

Gwyn envied them the noise, the arguments, even the crying. He came upon a similar scene every morning, and it never failed to make him feel separate and alone. Sometimes he would hang behind just watching, reluctant to intrude.

Today, however, Gwyn had something to announce. Today he did not feel alone. Different, yes, but not awkward and excluded.

"Alun! Alun!" he shouted. "I've got news for you."

Alun swung around, lowering Iolo to the ground. The other Lloyds looked up as Gwyn came flying down the lane.

"Go on," said Alun. "What news?"

"I'm a magician," cried Gwyn. "A magician." And he ran past them, his arms outstretched triumphantly, his satchel banging on his back.

"A magician," scoffed Alun. "You're mad, Gwyn Griffiths, that's what you are." Forgetting his duty, he left Iolo on the lane and gave furious chase.

"Mad! Mad!" echoed Siôn and Gareth, following Alun's example.

"Mad! Mad!" cried Iolo excitedly, as he raced down the lane, away from his mother and his tears.

Soon there were four boys tearing neck and neck down the lane, and one not far behind. All were shouting, "Mad! Mad! Mad!" except for Gwyn, and he was laughing too much to say anything.

But the three girls, Nerys, Nia, and Kate, always impressed by their dark neighbor, stood quite still and murmured, "A magician?"

4

THE
SILVER SHIP

Nain had warned him that he would be alone, but Gwyn had not realized what that would mean. After all, he had felt himself to be alone ever since Bethan disappeared. But there had always been Alun to share a book or a game, to lend a sympathetic ear to confidences, to wander with on the mountain or in the woods.

And for Alun the need had also been great. Gwyn was the one with an empty house and a quiet space to think and play in. Gwyn was the clever one, the one to help with homework. It was Gwyn who had taught Alun to read. On winter evenings the two boys were seldom apart.

Gwyn had never imagined a time without Alun's friendship, and perhaps, if he had kept silent, that time would never have come. But it never occurred to

Gwyn that Alun would find it impossible to believe him. He felt that he only had to find the right words to convince his friend. So on the homeward journey that same afternoon, he again brought up the subject of magicians.

Iolo always raced ahead when they got off the school bus, but the older children were not so eager to run uphill. They lingered on the lane, Siôn and Gareth arguing, the girls collecting wildflowers or colored leaves. Alun and Gwyn always brought up the rear.

"Have you heard of Math, Lord of Gwynedd?" Gwyn began innocently.

"Of course. He's in the old Welsh stories. Dad talks about them," Alun replied.

"And Gwydion?"

"Yes, and how he made a ship from seaweed." Alun's interest had been aroused.

"I'd forgotten. Dad never talks. But Nain reminded me. She's got more books than I've seen anywhere, except in the library."

"Your Nain's a bit batty isn't she?" Alun had always been a little suspicious of Gwyn's grandmother.

"No! She's not batty! She knows a lot," Gwyn replied. "She knew about me, about my being a magician!"

"Now I know she's batty! And you are too," Alun said good-naturedly.

Gwyn stopped quite still. His words came slow and

quiet, not at all in the way he had intended. "I'm not mad. Things happened last night. I think I made them happen. . . . I wasn't dreaming. I saw my sister, or someone like my sister. Nain said Math and Gwydion were my ancestors . . . and that I have inherited . . ." He could not finish because Alun had begun to laugh.

"They're in stories. They're not real people. You can't be descended from a story!"

"You don't know. I can make the wind come. I saw another planet last night, very close. It was white and the buildings were white, and there was a tower with a silver bell." Gwyn was desperate to explain. "There were children. And this is the most fantastic part—I could hear them in a pipe that came from—"

"You're crazy! You're lying!" Alun cried bitterly. "Why are you lying? No one can see planets that close. They're millions and millions and millions of miles away!" He fled from Gwyn yelling, "Liar! Liar! Liar!"

"How d'you know, Alun Lloyd?" Gwyn called relentlessly. "You don't know anything, you don't. You're ignorant! I know what I know. And I know what I've seen!"

He had gone too far. Gwyn realized that even before Alun sprang through his gate and followed his brothers up the path to the house, slamming the door behind him to emphasize his distaste for Gwyn's conversation.

Gwyn was alone on the lane with Nerys, Nia, and Kate. The three girls had lost interest in their flowers

49

and were staring at Gwyn in dismay. He could not bring himself to speak, so he passed by in an awkward silence.

Half a mile further on he reached his grandmother's cottage. Knowing she was the only person in the world who would believe him, he unceremoniously burst in upon her. He was astonished at what he saw.

Nain had sewn up the red velvet dress. She was wearing it, standing in the center of her room like some exotic bird, surrounded by her flowering plants and gaudy paraphernalia. She had something shining on her forehead, huge rings on her fingers, and round her waist, a wide bronze chain.

"Nain!" said Gwyn, amazed. "Where are you going?"

"I'm staying here," his grandmother replied. "This is my castle. I have to defend it."

She was talking in riddles again. Gwyn decided to come straight to the point. "Nain, I got something else from the wind last night. A silver pipe. And there were voices in it, from far away."

"Ah," said Nain. "Even when men whispered, Math could hear them. He could hear voices beyond any mortal ear! The pipe is from him!"

"And something happened," Gwyn went on, "in Arianwen's web!"

His grandmother began to move about her room, but Gwyn knew she was listening to his story. When he mentioned the girl in the web, she stopped in front of a huge gilt-framed mirror at the back of the room and said softly, "Gwydion Gwyn, you will soon have your heart's desire!"

"My heart's desire?" repeated Gwyn. "I believe I am a magician, but I'm not strong yet. I don't know if these things are happening to me because I have the power, or if they would have happened to anyone."

"You've forgotten the legends, haven't you, poor boy?" said Nain. "I used to read them to you long ago, but your father stopped all that when Bethan went. He stopped all the fun, all the joy. But he couldn't stop you, could he? Because you are who you are. Now I'll read you something."

In spite of the multitude of books scattered about the room, his grandmother always knew exactly where to find the one she needed. From beneath a blue china dog that supported a lopsided lampshade, she withdrew a huge black book, its leather cover scarred with age.

"The legends," she purred, stroking the battered spine. It looked so awesome and so old Gwyn half expected a cloud of bats to fly out when his grandmother opened it.

She furled the train of her velvet dress around her legs, settled herself on a pile of cushions, and beckoned to him.

Gwyn peered at the book over his grandmother's shoulder. "It's in old Welsh," he complained. "I can't understand it."

"Huh!" she sighed. "I forgot. Listen, I'll translate.

'At dawn rose Gwydion, the magician, before the cock crowed, and he summoned to him his power and his magic, and he went to the sea and found dulse and seaweed, and he held it close and spoke to it, then cast it out over the sea, and there appeared the most marvellous ship. . . .' " She turned the next few pages hurriedly, anxious to find the words that would convey to Gwyn what she wanted. "Ah, here," she exclaimed. "Now you will understand. 'Then Gwydion's son subdued the land and ruled over it prosperously, and thereafter he became Lord over Gwynedd!' " She closed the book triumphantly.

"Well?" said Gwyn. "I don't think I understand, yet."

"He was our ancestor, that Lord of Gwynedd," said Nain, "and so, it follows, was Gwydion."

"But they're in a story, Nain." In spite of himself Gwyn found himself repeating Alun's words. "They're not real people."

"Not real?" Nain rose tall and proud out of her chair. "They're our ancestors," she said, glaring at Gwyn and slamming the book down on top of others piled on the table beside her.

Gwyn winced as a cloud of dust flew into his face. A tiny jug tottered precariously beside the books, fortunately coming to rest before it reached the edge of the table.

"But how do you know, Nain?" he persisted quietly.

"How do I know? How do I know? Listen!" Nain

settled back onto the cushions and drew Gwyn down beside her. "My great-great-grandmother told me. She was a hundred years old and I was ten, and I believed her. And now I'll tell you something I've never told anyone, not even your father. She was a witch, my great-great-grandmother. She gave me the seaweed and the brooch and the whistle. 'Keep it for you-know-who,' she said, and I did know who."

"And the broken horse?"

Nain frowned. "I am afraid of that horse," she said thoughtfully. "I tried to burn it once, but I couldn't. It was still there when the fire died, black and grinning at me. I believe it is a dreadful thing, and she thought so too, my great-great-grandmother. She tied a label on it, '*Dim hon!* Not this!' for it must never be used, ever. It must be kept safe, locked away. Tight, tight, tight. It is old and evil."

"I'll keep it safe, Nain. But what about the scarf? She didn't give you the scarf, your great-great-grand-mother?"

"No, not the scarf. That was my idea. I found it on the mountain, the morning after Bethan went. But I didn't tell a soul. What would have been the use? I kept it for you."

"Why for me?"

"Can't you guess? I knew you would need it."

"And are you a witch too, Nain?" Gwyn ventured.

"No," Nain shook her head regretfully. "I haven't the power. I've tried, but it hasn't come to me."

"And how do you know it has come to me?"

"Ah, I knew when you were born. It was All Hallows Day, don't forget, the beginning of the Celtic New Year. Such a bright dawn it was, all the birds in the world were singing. Like bells wasn't it? Bells ringing in the air. Your father came flying down the lane. 'The baby's on the way, Mam,' he cried. He was so anxious, so excited. By the time we got back to the house you were nearly in this world. And when you came, and I saw your eyes so bright, I knew. And little Bethan knew too, although she was only five. She was such a strange one, so knowing yet so wild. Sometimes I thought she was hardly of this world. But how she loved you! And your dad, so proud he was. What a morning!"

"He doesn't even like me now," Gwyn murmured.

"No, and that's what we have to change, isn't it?" Nain said gently.

Gwyn buried his face in his hands. "Oh, I don't know! I don't know!" he cried. "How can a spider and a pipe help me? And what has another world to do with Bethan? I've just had a fight with my best friend. He wouldn't believe me."

"I warned you never to betray your secret," Nain admonished him. "Never abuse your power. You must be alone if you are to achieve your heart's desire."

"What's the use of magic if no one knows about it?" Gwyn exclaimed irritably. "And how do I get my heart's desire?"

54

"You know very well," Nain replied unhelpfully. "Think about the scarf. Think about using it. And now you'd better leave me and eat the supper that is growing cold on your mother's table."

The room had become dark without their noticing it. The fire had almost died, and the few remaining embers glowed like tiny jewels in the grate. Gwyn was unwilling to leave. He wanted to talk on into the night. But Nain was not of the same mind, it seemed. She lit a lamp and began to pace about her room, moving books and ornaments in a disturbed and thoughtless manner, as though she was trying either to forget or to remember something.

Gwyn pulled himself up from the pile of cushions and moved to the door. "Good night then, Nain!" he said.

The tall figure, all red and gold in the lamplight, did not even turn towards him. But when he reluctantly slipped out into the night, words came singing after him: "*Cysgwch yn dawel*, Gwydion Gwyn! Sleep quietly!"

When he got home, the table was bare.

"Did your grandmother give you a meal?" his mother inquired, guessing where he had been.

"No," said Gwyn. "I forgot to ask."

Mrs. Griffiths smiled. "What a one you are!" She gave him a plate of stew that had been kept warm on the stove.

Gwyn could not finish the meal. He went upstairs early, muttering about homework.

He did not sleep soundly. It was a strange, wild night. The restless apple tree beneath his window disturbed him. He dreamed of Nain, tall for a ten-year-old, in a red dress, her black curls tied with a scarlet ribbon. She was listening to her great-great-grandmother, an old woman, a witch, with long gray hair and wrinkled hands clasped in her dark lap, where a piece of seaweed lay, all soft and shining, as though it was still moving in water, not stranded on the knees of an old woman.

Gwyn gasped. He sat up, stiff and terrified. He felt for the bedside light and turned it on.

Arianwen was sitting on the silver pipe. Gwyn lifted the pipe until it was close to his face. He stared at the spider and the pipe, willing them to work for him. But they did not respond. He laid them carefully on the bedside table and got out of bed.

His black watch told him that it was four o'clock—not yet dawn. He dressed and opened his top drawer. It was time for the seaweed. But instead, he took out Bethan's yellow scarf and, without knowing why, wrapped it slowly round his neck, pressing it to his face and inhaling the musty sweet smell of roses. He closed his eyes and for a moment almost thought that he was close to an answer. But he had forgotten the question. It was something his grandmother had said—something about using the scarf. Try as he might to order his mind, he felt the answer and the question slipping away from him, until he was left with only the tangible effects: the scarf and the dry dusty stick of seaweed.

Gwyn tucked the seaweed into the pocket of his coat and went downstairs, letting himself out of the back door into the yard.

There was a pale light in the sky, but the birds were still at rest. The only sounds came from sheep moving on the hard mountain earth and frosty hedgerows shivering in the cold air.

He did not ascend the mountain this time, but wandered northwards, through the lower slopes, seeking the breeze that came from the sea. Here the land was steep and barren. There were few sheep, no trees, and no farms. Gigantic rocks thrust their way through the earth, and torrents of ice-cold water tumbled over the stones. Gwyn longed for the comfort of a wall to cling to. The wide, dark space of empty land and sky threatened to sweep him away and swallow him. One step missed, he thought, and he would slip into nowhere.

And then he smelled the sea. Moonlight became dawn, and colors appeared on the mountain. He was approaching the gentler western slopes. He started to climb upwards field by field, keeping close to the stone walls, so that the breeze that had now veered into a wailing northeast wind would not confuse his steps.

Gwyn had passed the fields and was standing in the center of a steep stretch of bracken when it happened. The thing in his pocket began to move and slide through his fingers, causing him to withdraw his hand and regard the soft purple fronds of what had, a few moments before, been a dried-up piece of seaweed. The transformation was unbelievable. Gwyn held the plant out before him and the slippery petallike shapes flapped in the wind like a hovering bird. And then it was gone. The wind blew it out of his hand and out to sea. All the birds above and below him awoke and called out. The gray sky was pierced with light, and in that moment Gwyn knew what he had to do.

He took off the yellow scarf and flung it out to the sky, calling his sister's name again and again over the wind, over the brightening land and the upturned faces of startled sheep.

Then, from the west, where it was still dark and where the water was still black under the heavy clouds, there came a light. Tiny at first, but growing as it fell towards the sea. It was a cool light, soft and silver. As it came closer, Gwyn could make out the shape of a billowing sail, and the bow of a great ship. But the ship was not upon the sea. It was in the air above the sea, rising all the time, until it was opposite him and approaching the mountain.

A wave of ice-cold air suddenly hit Gwyn's body, throwing him back into the bracken. As he lay there, shocked and staring upwards, the huge hull of the silver ship passed right over him, and he could see fragments of ice, like sparks, falling away from it. He could see

58

patterns of flowers and strange creatures engraved in the silver, and then the ice was in his eyes and he had to close them. He curled himself into a ball, shaking with the pain of bitter cold that enveloped him.

A dull thud shook the ground. Something scraped across the rocks and filled the air with a sigh.

Gwyn lay hidden in the bracken for a long time, curled up tight with eyes closed, too frightened and amazed to move. When he finally stood up, the freezing cold air was gone. He looked behind him, around and above him, but the mountain was empty. There was snow on the bracken and in one flat field beyond the bracken, but there was no sign of a ship of any kind. Yet he had seen one, heard one, felt the bitter cold of its passage through the air.

Gwyn began to run. Now that it was light, he had no difficulty finding his way across the northern slopes. Soon he was back in familiar fields. But when he came to within sight of Tŷ Bryn, he paused a moment, then kept on running, down the track, past his gate, past his grandmother's cottage, until he reached the Lloyds' farmhouse. He flung open the gate, rushed up the path and, ignoring the bell, beat upon the door with his fists, shouting, "Alun! Alun! Come quick! I want to tell you something! Now! Now! Now!"

Within the house someone shouted angrily. It must have been Mr. Lloyd. Then there were footsteps pattering on the stairs and down the hallway.

The front door opened and Mrs. Lloyd stood there in a pink bathrobe, with rollers in her hair and her face all red and shiny.

"Whatever is it, Gwyn Griffiths?" she said. "Accident or fire?"

"No fire, Mrs. Lloyd. I want Alun. I have to tell him something. It's urgent!"

"No fire, no accident," snapped Mrs. Lloyd. "Then what are you doing here? We've not had breakfast. Why can't it wait till school?"

"Because it's just happened!" Gwyn stamped his foot impatiently. "I've got to see Alun."

Mrs. Lloyd was angry. She seemed about to send Gwyn away, but something in the boy standing tense and dark against the dawn clouds made her hesitate. "Alun! You'd better come down," she called. "It's Gwyn Griffiths. I don't know what it's about, but you'd better come."

"Shut that door," Mr. Lloyd shouted from above. "I can feel the cold up here."

"Come inside and wait!" Mrs. Lloyd pulled Gwyn into the house and shut the door. "I don't know— you've got a nerve these days, you boys."

She shuffled into the kitchen, leaving Gwyn alone in the shadows by the door. It was cold in the Lloyds' house. The narrow hall was crammed with bicycles, boots, coats half-hanging on hooks. It was carpeted with odd gloves, felt-tip pens, comics, and broken toys, and there were two pairs of muddy jeans hanging on the bannisters.

Alun appeared at the top of the stairs in pajamas that were too small. He was trying to reduce the cold gap round his stomach with one hand, while rubbing his eyes with the other. "What is it?" he asked sleepily.

"Come down here," Gwyn whispered. "Come closer."

Alun trudged down reluctantly and approached Gwyn. "Tell, then," he said.

Gwyn took a breath. He tried to choose the right words, so that Alun would believe what he said. "I've been on the mountain. I couldn't sleep, so I went for a look at the sea. . . ."

"In the dark?" Alun was impressed. "You're brave. I couldn't do that."

"There was a moon. It was quite bright really," Gwyn paused. "Anyway, while I was there I . . . I . . ."

"Go on!" Alun yawned and clutched his stomach, thinking of warm porridge.

"Well—you've got to believe me"—Gwyn hesitated dramatically—"I saw a spaceship!" He waited for a response, but none came.

"What?" Alun said at last.

"I saw a ship . . . fall out of space. It came right over the sea. . . . It was silver and had a sort of sail . . . and it was cold, ever so cold. I couldn't breathe with the cold of it. I had to lie all curled up, it hurt so much. And when I got up, it had gone!"

Alun remained silent. He stared at his bare toes and scratched his head.

"Do you believe me? Tell me!" Gwyn demanded. There was no reply.

"You don't believe me, do you?" Gwyn cried. "Why? *Why?*"

"Ssssh! They'll hear!" Alun said.

"So what?"

"They think you're a loony already."

"Do you? D'you think I'm a loony?" Gwyn asked fiercely. "I did see a ship. Why don't you believe me?"

"I don't know. It sounds impossible—a sail and all. Sounds silly. Spaceships aren't like that."

Gwyn felt defeated. Somehow he had used the wrong words. He would never make Alun believe, not like this, standing in a cold hallway before breakfast. "Well, don't believe me then," he said, "but don't tell either, will you? Don't tell anyone else."

"O.K.! O.K.!" said Alun. "You'd better go. Your mam'll be worried!"

"I'll go!" Gwyn opened the door and stepped onto the porch. But before Alun could shut him out, he said again, "You won't tell what I said, will you? It's important!"

Alun was so relieved at having rid himself of Gwyn's

disturbing presence, he did not notice the urgency in his friend's voice. "O.K.!" he said. "I've got to shut the door now, I'm freezing!"

5

EIRLYS

Alun did tell. He did not mean to hurt or ridicule Gwyn, and he only told one person. But that was enough.

The one person Alun told was Gary Pritchard. Gary Pritchard told his gang: Merfyn Jones, Dewi Davis, and Brian Roberts. Dewi Davis was the biggest tease in the class and within two days everyone in school had heard about Gwyn Griffiths and his "spaceship."

Little whispering groups were formed in the playground. There were murmurings in the cafeteria, and children watched while Gwyn ate in silence, staring steadily at his plate so that he would not meet their eyes. Girls giggled in the coatroom and even five-year-olds nudged each other when he passed.

And Gwyn made it easy for them. He never denied that he had seen a silver ship, nor did he try to explain or defend his story. He withdrew. He went to school, did his work, sat alone in the playground, and spoke to no one. He came home, fed the hens, and had a snack. He tried to respond to his mother's probing chatter without giving too much away, for he felt he had to protect her. He did not want her to know that his friends thought him crazy. But Mrs. Griffiths sensed something was wrong.

And then one evening Alun showed up. He had tried in vain to talk to Gwyn during their walks home from the bus, but since the gossiping began, Gwyn had deliberately avoided his old friend. He had run all the way home, passing the Lloyds on the lane, so that he would not hear them if they laughed.

Mrs. Griffiths was pleased to see Alun. She drew him into the kitchen saying, "Look who's here! We haven't seen you for a bit, Alun. Take your coat off!"

"No!" Gwyn leapt up and pushed Alun back into the hallway, slamming the kitchen door behind him. "What d'you want?" he asked suspiciously.

"Just a chat," said Alun nervously.

"What's there to chat about?"

"About the things you said. About the spaceship, and that," Alun replied, fingering the buttons on his coat.

"You don't believe, and you told," Gwyn said coldly.

"I know. I know and I'm sorry. I just wanted to talk about it." Alun sounded desperate.

"You want to spread more funny stories, I suppose."

"No . . . no," Alun said. "I just wanted to—"

"You can shove off," said Gwyn. He opened the front door and pushed Alun out on the porch. He caught a glimpse of Alun's white face under the porch light as he shut the door. "I'm busy," he called through the door, "so don't bother me again."

And he was busy, he and Arianwen. Every night she spun a web in the corner of Gwyn's bedroom, between the end of the sloping ceiling and the cupboard. And there would always be something in the web. A tiny, faraway landscape, white and shining, or strange trees with icy leaves. Or a lake, or was it a sea? with ice floes bobbing on the water and a silver ship with sails like cobwebs, gliding over the surface.

And when he ran his fingers over the silver pipe he could hear waves breaking on the shore. He could hear icicles singing when the wind blew through the trees, and children's voices calling over the snow. And he knew beyond any shadow of a doubt that he was hearing sounds from another world.

Once Arianwen spun a larger cobweb again, covering an entire wall. The white tower appeared, and the same houses. Children came out to play in the square beneath the tower. Pale children with wonderfully serene faces, not shouting as earthbound children would have done, but calling in soft, musical voices. It began to snow, and suddenly all the children stood still and turned to look in the same direction. They looked right into the web. They looked at Gwyn and they smiled, and then they waved. It was as though someone had said, "Look, children! He's watching you! Wave to him!" And their bright eyes were so inviting Gwyn felt a longing to be with them, to be touched and soothed by them.

But who had told the children to turn? Gwyn realized he had never seen an adult in Arianwen's webs, never heard an adult voice. Who was looking after the faraway children? Perhaps they had just seen the "thing" that was sending the pictures down to Arianwen's web, a satellite perhaps, or a ship, another star, or another spider, whirling round in space. And they had turned to wave to it.

A few weeks before the end of the term, three new children appeared at school. They were children from the city, two boys from poor families who had no room for them, and a girl—an orphan it was said. They had all been put into the care of Mr. and Mrs. Herbert, a warmhearted couple with four girls, a large farmhouse, and an eagerness to help children less fortunate than their own.

John, Eirlys, and Dafydd were officially entering the school the following term, but had been allowed three weeks of settling in before the Christmas holidays. Miss Pugh, the principal, was a little put out. She had expected only two children, eight-year-old boys, to put in a class where there was still space for at least five more. There were thirty children in Gwyn's class, where

Eirlys would have to go. Mr. James, their teacher, a rather fastidious man, was already complaining that he could feel the children breathing on him. He gave Eirlys a tiny desk at the back of the class, where no one seemed to notice her.

In the excitement of Christmas preparations some of the children forgot about Gwyn and his "stories." But for Gary Pritchard and his gang, baiting Gwyn Griffiths was still more entertaining than anything else they could think of, especially when they saw a flicker of anger beginning to appear in their victim's dark eyes.

And then one Monday Dewi Davis went too far. It was a bright, cold day. Snow had fallen in the night, clean white snow that was kicked and muddied by children running into school. But snow fell again during the first lesson and, as luck would have it, stopped just before the first break. The children were presented with a beautiful white playground in which to slide and throw snowballs.

Dewi Davis could never resist a snowball, just as he could never resist shoving girls with white socks into puddles, or putting worms down the backs of squeamish classmates. He took a lot of trouble with Gwyn's snowball, patting and shaping it until it was rock-hard and as big as his own head. Then he followed Gwyn round the playground, as Gwyn, deep in thought, made patterns in the snow with his feet.

Soon Dewi had an audience. Children watched expectantly while Gwyn trudged unaware through the snow. Dewi stopped about three meters behind Gwyn and called in his slow lisping voice, "Hello, Mr. Magic. Seen any spaceships lately?"

Gwyn began to turn, but before he could see Dewi, the huge snowball hit him on the side of the face. A pain seared through his ear into his head.

Girls gasped and some giggled. Boys shouted and laughed, and someone said, "Go on, get him!"

Gwyn turned a full half circle and stared at Dewi Davis. He stared at his fat silly face and the grin on his thick pink lips, and he wanted to hurt him. He brought up his clenched right fist and thrust it out towards Dewi, opening his fingers wide as he did so. A low hiss came from within him, hardly belonging to him and not his voice at all, more like a wild animal.

There was nothing in Gwyn's hand, no stone, no snow. But something came out of his hand and hit Dewi in the middle of his face. He saw Dewi's nose grow and darken to purple, and saw hurt and amazement on Dewi's round face. Only he and Dewi knew that there had been nothing in his hand.

Then, suddenly, the rest of the gang were upon him. Someone hit him in the face, and someone else punched his stomach. His hair was tugged and his arms were jerked backwards until he screamed. And then his legs were pulled from under him, and he crashed onto the ground.

Everyone stopped shouting and stared at Gwyn, motionless in the mud and snow. The bell rang, and al-

69

most simultaneously, Dewi Davis began to scream for attention. The children drifted away as Mr. James ran to Dewi and helped him from the playground. The teacher never noticed Gwyn lying in a corner.

The whole of Gwyn's body ached, but his head hurt most of all. He could not get up and did not want to. There was blood on the snow beside him, and his lip felt swollen and sticky. The playground was empty. He wondered if he would have to lie there all day. Perhaps the snow would fall again and no one would see him until it was time to go home. He managed to pull himself up until he was kneeling on all fours, but it was an effort. He could not get any further because something in his back hurt whenever he moved.

And then he saw that he was not alone. Someone was standing on the other side of the playground. Someone in gray with long, fair hair and a blue hat. It was Eirlys. The girl began to walk towards Gwyn slowly, as though she was approaching a creature she did not wish to alarm. When she reached Gwyn she bent down and put her arms around his body. Then, without a word, she lifted him to his feet. She was very frail, and Gwyn could not understand where her strength came from. Her hair was so soft it was like touching water, and her face, close to his, was almost as pale as the snow. He had never really looked at her before. Now he realized with a shock that he knew her. He had seen her somewhere but could not remember where.

They walked across the playground together, still

without speaking, his arms resting on her shoulders, her arm round his waist. Although his legs ached, he tried not to stumble or lean too heavily on the girl. When they reached the school door, Eirlys withdrew her arm and then took his hand from her shoulder. Her fingers were ice-cold. Gwyn gasped when she touched his hand.

"What is it?" she asked.

"You're so cold," he replied.

Eirlys smiled. Her eyes were greeny blue, like arctic water. It was as though they had once been another color, but that other color had been washed away.

When they got to the classroom Gwyn told Mr. James that he had slipped in the snow. Eirlys said nothing. Mr. James nodded. "Get on with your work now," he said.

Eirlys and Gwyn went to their desks. Everyone stared. Dewi Davis was still holding his nose, and Gwyn remembered what he had done. All through the next lesson, through the pain in his head, he kept thinking of what he had done to Dewi Davis. He had hit him with magic. Something had come out of his hand and flown into Dewi's face, something that had come to him from Gwydion, the magician, and from Gwydion's son, who had once ruled Gwynedd. And it was the same thing that had turned the seaweed into a ship, the brooch into a spider, and the whistle into a silver pipe. These last three, he realized, had merely been waiting for him to release them. They had been there all the time, just waiting for his call. But when he had hit Dewi Davis, he had done it by himself. He had wanted to hurt Dewi, to smash his silly, cruel face, and he had done it, not with a stone nor with his fist, but with his will and the power that had come from Gwydion. If he could do that, what could he not do?

While Gwyn dreamed over his desk, he was unaware of Eirlys watching him. But Alun Lloyd noticed, and he wondered why the girl gazed at Gwyn with her aquamarine eyes. Alun was uneasy.

During the day Gwyn's aches and pains receded, and he was able to hobble to the school bus unaided. When he got off the bus, however, he could not run up the lane, and he felt trapped. Alun was lingering behind the rest of his family, watching him.

"You O.K.?" Alun asked Gwyn.

"Yes, I'm O.K."

"D'you want me to walk up with you?"

"No," Gwyn replied. "I said I was all right, didn't I?"

"Are you sure?" Alun persisted. He turned to face Gwyn and began to walk up the hill backwards.

"They didn't hurt me that bad," Gwyn said angrily. "I just can't walk that fast."

"I suppose she's going to help you?" Alun said. He was still walking backwards and looking at someone behind Gwyn.

"Who?"

"Her!" Alun nodded in the direction of the main road. Then he turned and ran up the lane.

Gwyn glanced over his shoulder to see what Alun had meant. Eirlys was walking up towards him.

"What are you doing?" Gwyn shouted. "You don't get off here!"

The girl just smiled and kept coming.

"You'll be in trouble! How're you going to get home?"

"I'll walk," said Eirlys.

"Oh heck!" cried Gwyn.

"Don't worry!" The girl continued her approach and Gwyn waited, unable to turn his back on her.

"It'll be all right," she said when she was beside him. "I'll just come home with you. You might need someone, with all those bruises." She tapped his arm and went ahead up the hill.

When they turned a bend and Nain's cottage suddenly came into view, Eirlys stopped and stared at the building.

"My grandmother lives there," Gwyn said.

"Does she." Eirlys spoke the words not as a question, but as a response that was expected of her.

She passed the cottage slowly, trailing her fingers along the top of the stone wall. Sprays of snow flew onto her sleeve, and she never took her eyes off the light in Nain's downstairs window.

Gwyn was tempted to take the girl in to meet his

grandmother. But it was getting dark, and they still had to pass the furrows of snow that had drifted into the narrow path further on. He wondered how on earth Eirlys was going to get home. "What will Mrs. . . . What's-'er-name say, when you're not on the bus?" he asked.

"Mrs. Herbert? She's kind. She'll understand," Eirlys replied.

They held hands when they reached the snowdrifts, Gwyn leading the girl to higher ground at the edge of the path. Once again he gasped at the icy touch of her fingers, and when Eirlys laughed, the sound was familiar to him.

She was reluctant to come into the farmhouse, and when Gwyn insisted, she approached it cautiously, with a puzzled frown on her face. Every now and then she would look away from the house, up to where the mountain should have been, but where, now, only a moving white mist could be seen.

"Come on," said Gwyn. "Mam'll give you a cup of tea."

He opened the front door and called into the kitchen, "I'm back, Mam. Sorry I'm late. I had a bit of trouble with the snow."

"I thought you would," came the reply.

His mother was stirring something on the stove when he went into the kitchen. She turned to speak to him but instead cried out, "Your face! What's happened?"

74

"I had a bit of a fight. It's not anything, really!" Gwyn said.

His father got up from the chair by the kitchen table, where he had been mending some electrical equipment. He was about to be angry, but then he saw Eirlys standing in the doorway. "Who's this?" he asked.

"Eirlys!" said Gwyn. "She helped me. She walked up from the bus with me to see I was all right."

"That was kind of you, Eirlys," said Mrs. Griffiths. "Take your coat off and warm up a bit. I'll make a pot of tea."

She began to help Gwyn with his coat, exclaiming all the time at the state of his muddy clothes and the bruises on his face.

Eirlys came into the room and took off her hat and coat. She drew a chair up to the table and sat down opposite Mr. Griffiths. He just stood there, staring at her, while his big hands groped for the tiny brass screws that had escaped him and now spun out across the table.

The girl caught one of the screws and stretched across to put it safe into his hand. Gwyn heard the sharp intake of breath as his father felt her icy fingers. He laughed. "She's cold-blooded, isn't she, Dad?" he said.

Mr. Griffiths did not reply. He sat down and began his work again. Mrs. Griffiths poured the tea and brought a fruit cake to the table. They discussed the snow and the school and the fight. Mrs. Griffiths asked how and why the fight had begun. Although Gwyn could not give a satisfactory explanation, Mr. Griffiths did not say a word. He did not even seem to be listening to them, but every now and then he would look up and stare at Eirlys.

When it was dark Mrs. Griffiths said, "You'd better ring your mam, she'll be worrying."

"She hasn't got a mam," Gwyn answered for the girl. "She's living with the Herberts."

"Oh, you poor love." Mrs. Griffiths shook her head sympathetically.

"They're lovely," said Eirlys brightly, "so kind. They won't mind. They'll fetch me. They said they always would if I wanted, and it's not far."

"No need for that." Mr. Griffiths suddenly stood up. "I'll take you in the Land Rover."

Gwyn was amazed. His father never offered lifts. "You're honored," he whispered to Eirlys as Mr. Griffiths strode out of the back door.

By the time Eirlys had gathered up her hat and coat and her schoolbag, the deep throbbing of the Land Rover's engine could be heard out in the lane.

"Good-bye," said Eirlys. She walked up to Mrs. Griffiths and kissed her. Mrs. Griffiths was startled. She looked as though she had seen a ghost.

She remained in the kitchen while Gwyn and the girl walked down to the gate. The door of the Land Rover was open, and Mr. Griffiths was standing beside it. "You'll have to get in this side and climb over," he told Eirlys, "the snow's deep on the other side."

Gwyn had never known his father to be so considerate to a child.

Eirlys stepped out into the lane, but before she could climb into the Land Rover, Mr. Griffiths' arms were around her, helping her up. For a second the two shadowy figures became one and, for some reason, Gwyn felt that he did not belong to the scene. He looked away to the frozen hedges glittering in the glare of the headlights.

Inside the house the telephone began to ring. Then the Land Rover's wheels spun, and Gwyn had to back away from the sprays of wet snow. It was too late to shout good-bye.

He turned to go back into the house and saw his mother standing on the porch. "Mrs. Davis, Tŷ Coch, was on the phone," she said gravely. "She wants to talk to us tomorrow. It's about Dewi's nose!"

6

A DROWNING

"We've left Dewi with his auntie," said Mrs. Davis.
Dewi had many aunties. Gwyn wondered which one had the pleasure of his company, and if Dewi was to be envied or pitied.

The Davises had come to "thrash out the problem of the nose," as Mr. Davis put it.

It was six o'clock. The tea had only just been cleared away, and Gwyn's stomach was already grumbling. Mr. and Mrs. Davis, Gwyn, and his parents were sitting around the kitchen table as though they were about to embark on an evening of cards or some other lighthearted entertainment, not something as serious as Dewi's nose.

"The problem, as I see it," began Mrs. Davis, "is, who's lying?"

"Gary Pritchard, Merfyn Jones, *and* Brian Roberts, all say that they think they saw Gwyn throw a stone," said Mr. Davis solemnly. "Now, this is a very serious business."

"Very dangerous too," added Mrs. Davis.

"That goes without saying, Gladys." Mr. Davis coughed. "Now, the situation is," he paused dramatically, "what's to be done about it?"

"How . . . er, how bad is the nose?" Mrs. Griffiths asked.

"Very bad," replied Mrs. Davis indignantly. "How bad d'you think your nose would be if it had been hit by a rock?"

"Now wait a minute!" Mr. Griffiths entered the conversation with a roar. "First it's a stone, now it's a rock, and we haven't yet established whether *anything* was thrown. Perhaps Dewi bumped his nose. We haven't heard *his* explanation."

"That's the problem." Mr. Davis banged his fist on the table. "Dewi says he did bump his nose, but the other boys say Gwyn hit him with a stone."

"Dewi's frightened of him, see!" Mrs. Davis pointed an accusing finger at Gwyn. "He's afraid your boy'll do something worse to him if he tells."

"Bloody nonsense!" Mr. Griffiths stood up, his chair scraping on the tiled floor. "Let's hear your side of it, Gwyn."

Gwyn looked up. He was unused to having his father defend him. He felt that he could take on any number of Davises now. "I didn't throw a stone," he said.

"There!" Mr. and Mrs. Davis spoke simultaneously.

Mr. Griffiths sat down and the two sets of parents eyed each other wordlessly.

"He's lying, of course," Mr. Davis said at last.

"He ought to be punished," added his wife. "The principal should be told."

"It's a pity they don't thrash kids these days," growled Mr. Davis.

This time it was Mr. Griffiths who banged the table. Gwyn got up and began to pace about the room while the adults all talked at once. He had a tremendous desire to do something dramatic, and the knowledge that he probably could made the temptation almost unbearable. What should he do though? Box Mr. Davis's ears from a distance of three meters? Pull Mrs. Davis's hair? The possibilities were endless. And then he remembered Nain's warning. He must not abuse his power. It must be used only when there was something that he truly needed to do.

"It's not as if your son is normal," he heard Mrs. Davis say. "Everyone's been talking about his being *peculiar*, if you know what I mean. Ask any of the children."

For the first time his parents seemed unable to reply. Mrs. Griffiths looked so miserable that Gwyn could hardly bear it. She had known for days that something was wrong, and now she was going to hear about his "stories."

"It seems," Mrs. Davis went on, "that Gwyn has been saying some very *peculiar* things, if you know what I mean. And why? If you ask me, your son's not normal."

Gwyn had to stop her. Contemplating the generous curves that overflowed the narrow kitchen chair supporting Mrs. Davis, his eyes alighted upon a large expanse of flesh just above her knee that her too-tight skirt could not cover. He flexed his fingers, pressed his thumb and forefinger together tight, tight, tight!

Mrs. Davis screamed. She glared at Mr. Griffiths and then asked haughtily, "Have you got a dog?"

The two men frowned at her and then frowned at each other. Mrs. Griffiths said, "Yes, he's in the barn."

"A cat?" Mrs. Davis inquired hopefully.

"A black tom." Mrs. Griffiths nodded towards a dark form sitting on the sill outside the kitchen window. "We call him Long John," she said, "because he lost a leg on the road when he was just a kitten. It's wonderful what vets can do these days."

Mrs. Davis glanced at Long John and then quickly looked away, her pink lips contorted with distaste. "I think we'll go," she said and stood up.

Her husband looked at her but did not move.

"Get up, Bryn!" Mrs. Davis commanded. "I want to go!"

Mr. Davis followed his wife out of the kitchen with

a perplexed expression on his face, as though he could not understand why the interview had ended so abruptly and wondered if the situation had been resolved without his being aware of it.

Mr. and Mrs. Griffiths were as perplexed as he. They silently followed their unwelcome guests to the front door. There the whole unpleasant business might have ended, had not Mrs. Davis been heard to mutter darkly, "Someone pinched my thigh!"

Mrs. Griffiths gasped. Her husband roared "What?" But Mr. Davis, having opened the front door, thrust his wife through it before she could cause the affair to deteriorate further. He then followed quickly after her, and the wind parted the two families by slamming the door.

Mr. and Mrs. Griffiths retreated into the kitchen and slumped battle-weary beside the table. Then the humor of the situation overcame them and they began to laugh with relief.

"Thanks for sticking up for me, Dad," said Gwyn, when his parents had recovered. He felt awkward and not at all sure that he had done the right thing in the end.

"If you say you're innocent, that's all I need to know," said Mr. Griffiths gruffly.

Gwyn looked hard at his father. He could not understand this change of attitude. A week ago his father would neither have believed nor defended him. In all probability he would have been sentenced to a week-end in his room and a meal of bread and water. "I'd better get on with my homework," he said shyly.

He was about to leave the room when his father suddenly said, "Is that girl coming again, then?"

"What girl?" Gwyn asked.

"You know what girl. The one that was here yesterday. I can always run her home if . . ." his father hesitated and then added diffidently, "if she wants to come."

"I don't suppose she will," said Gwyn. "She's a girl. She only came because I was hurt."

"Oh, that was it?"

Gwyn thought he could detect something almost like regret in his father's voice. What had come over the man? It was quite disturbing. It had nothing to do with himself, Gwyn was sure of that. He knew, instinctively, that he could not, should not, use his power to influence thought.

The pinch had been satisfactory though.

Gwyn realized that his father's mood had changed when Eirlys appeared. If that was the case, then she would have to come again, if only to keep his father happy. And so, although it was against his principles to have girls at Tŷ Bryn, the following day he asked Eirlys if she could come to the farm on Saturday.

"Of course," Eirlys replied. Her eyes shone with pleasure.

"Mam and Dad want it," said Gwyn, by way of explanation, "and . . . and so do I, of course!"

The weather changed. December brought sun instead of snow. The wind was warm and smelled of damp leaves and overripe apples.

Gwyn took Eirlys on his mountain, and she saw it in sunshine. Before she had only glimpsed it at dusk, through a mist of snow. Now she saw the colors that he loved, the buzzards hunting low over the fields, the rosy clouds drifting above the plateau. Gwyn had not realized that he would enjoy the company of a girl. But then Eirlys was not like other girls.

They leaped and sometimes slipped upon wet stones in the tumbling streams. They ran, arms outstretched, along the stone walls, scattering the sheep that dozed there. They chased crows that hopped like black thieves behind the leafless trees. And somehow Gwyn's father always seemed to be there, watching them from a distance or walking nearby with his dog and his blackthorn stick, listening to their voices. After tea he began to whistle in his workshop, and Gwyn realized he hardly recognized the sound. Even his mother looked up, astonished, from her ironing.

In the evening, while it was still light enough to see the trees, the children walked in the orchard. Gwyn told Eirlys about Nain and the five gifts, about the power that had come to him from Gwydion, and how he had hit Dewi Davis without a stone. He told her about the silver ship that had caused all his trouble at school. Unlike Alun, Eirlys believed him. She did not think it strange that a ship had fallen out of the sky. Even so, Gwyn did not mention the snow spider. He was still wary of confiding too much. "I'll take you to see my grandmother," he told the girl. Nain would know whether he could tell Eirlys about the cobwebs.

Later, he asked his parents if Eirlys could come again, so that they could visit Nain.

"Why can't she stay the night?" Mr. Griffiths suggested. "She can sleep in Bethan's room."

"No!" cried Mrs. Griffiths. And then more quietly she added, "It's . . . it's just that the room isn't ready!"

Nothing more was said just then, but when Mr. Griffiths had returned from his trip to the Herberts he suddenly remarked, "Shall we ask the girl for Christmas? She can stay a day or two, and there'll be time to get the room ready."

"No!" his wife said again. "No! It's my Bethan's room."

"But she isn't here, Mam," Gwyn said gently.

"It's waiting for her, though," his mother reproached him.

"But Eirlys could *sleep* there," Gwyn persisted. "The room *is* ready—I looked in. The bed is made, and the patchwork quilt is on it. The cupboards are shiny and all the dolls are there. It's such a waste!"

"Yes, all the dolls are there!" cried Mrs. Griffiths.

She sank into a chair and bent her head, covering her face with her hands. "You don't seem to care anymore, either of you. It's my daughter's room, my Bethan's. Her bed, her dolls, her place."

Her husband and her son stood watching her, sad and helpless. How could they tell her that it did not matter if Bethan was not with them, because now there was Eirlys?

"We won't discuss it now," said Mr. Griffiths. "But I've already agreed to fetch the girl tomorrow. Be kind while she's here. She's an orphan, remember."

"I won't upset her," Mrs. Griffiths said. "I'm sorry for her. She's just not my Bethan."

When Gwyn took Eirlys to visit his grandmother the following afternoon, Nain was waiting by the gate. She had dressed carefully for the occasion in an emerald green dress and scarlet stockings. Round her neck she wore a rope of grass green beads long enough to touch the silver buckle on her belt. From each ear swung a tiny golden cage with a silver bird tinkling inside it.

Eirlys was most impressed. "How beautiful you look," she said, and won Nain's heart.

Gwyn noticed that his grandmother could not take her eyes off the girl. She watched her every move, hungrily, like a bright-eyed cat might watch a bird. "*Eirlys!*" she murmured, "that's Welsh for 'snowdrop'. So we have a snowflower among us!"

After they had sipped their tea and eaten cake that tasted of cinnamon and rosemary, Gwyn told his grandmother about the ship and about Dewi Davis's nose. Eirlys wandered round the room, touching the china, the beads, and the plants. She studied the pictures in the dusty books and tied colored scarves around her head.

Nain was not surprised to hear about the silver ship. She merely nodded and said, "Ah, yes! You have nearly reached what you wanted, Gwydion Gwyn. But be careful! Don't do anything foolish!"

"Shall I tell Eirlys about the spider?" Gwyn asked his grandmother. "Should she know about the cobwebs and that other world?"

"Of course," said Nain, "though I believe she knows already."

They left the cottage before dark. Nain followed them to the gate, and as they set off up the path she called again, "Be careful!"

Gwyn was not listening to his grandmother. He had begun to tell Eirlys about the spider. He realized that he had not seen Arianwen for several days and wondered where she was.

When they got back to the farmhouse, Mrs. Griffiths was upstairs, sewing the hem on her new bedroom curtains. Her husband was cleaning the Land Rover. He had used it to transport a new batch of pullets from the Lloyds' that morning, and they had made more of a mess than he had bargained for.

Gwyn told Eirlys to wait in the kitchen while he fetched the pipe and the spider from his attic room. When he returned she was sitting in the armchair by the stove. The light was fading, but a tiny slither of winter sun had crept through the swaying branches of the apple tree and into the kitchen window. The light glimmered on the girl in the armchair, and Gwyn had to stop and take a breath before he said, "You are the girl in the web, Eirlys!"

"Am I?" she said.

"Yes, it was you! I knew it all the time, but I couldn't see how. . . . You're like my sister, too. Where have you come from, Eirlys?"

The girl just smiled her inscrutable smile and asked, "Where is the spider?"

"I don't know," he replied. "I looked in the drawer, on top of the cupboard, and under the bed. I couldn't find her."

Eirlys looked concerned. "Where can she be?"

Gwyn shrugged. "I don't know. She's been gone before, but only for a day. I haven't seen her for nearly a week."

His father called through the front door, "Time to go, Eirlys. Are you ready?"

Eirlys stood up. "You must find the spider, Gwyn," she said. "She's precious! She will make it possible for you to see whatever you want, and when I—"

"When you what?" Gwyn demanded.

"I can't say, just yet," Eirlys replied. And then she

disappeared into the hallway and ran out of the house before Gwyn had time to think of another question.

He watched the lights of the Land Rover flickering on the lane and then went upstairs to his room. This time he shook the curtains, felt under the carpet and, beginning to panic, emptied the contents of every drawer onto the floor. Arianwen was not there.

He went down to the kitchen to see his mother. "Have you seen that spider?" he inquired.

"I've seen too many spiders," Mrs. Griffiths replied. She was rolling pastry on the kitchen table and did not look up when she spoke.

"But have you seen my own particular spider?"

"I saw one, yes. It could have been the one." Mrs. Griffiths rolled and rolled the pastry without even a glance toward Gwyn. "It was different," she went on, "a sort of gray."

"Silver!" Gwyn corrected her. "Where was it?"

"Here. On the curtain."

"Did you catch it?"

"Yes! You know I can't abide cobwebs." Mrs. Griffiths had finished the pastry, but still she did not look up.

"What did you do with it?"

"I put it down the drain," his mother said flatly. "Drowned it!"

Gwyn was speechless. He could not believe what he had heard. His mother had to be joking. He stared at her, hoping for a smile or a teasing word, but she kept tearing little pieces away from the pastry and would not meet his eyes.

And then Gwyn found himself screaming, "Drowned? Drowned? You can't have done that!"

"Well, I did!" At last his mother faced him. "You know I don't like spiders. Why did you keep it so long?" She could not explain to Gwyn that she was afraid, not only of the spider, but of the strange girl who could not be her daughter, yet seemed so like her, and who was beginning to take her daughter's place.

"You don't understand," Gwyn cried. "You don't know what you've done!" He ran to the kitchen sink. "Did you put it down here? Where does the drain go to?"

"The septic tank," Mrs. Griffiths said defiantly. Guilt was making her angry. "And you can't look there. Nothing can live in that stuff. The spider's dead."

7

THE
BROKEN HORSE

"No! No! No!" Gwyn rushed out of the kitchen and up to his room. He regarded the dark places where cobwebs had sparkled with snow from that other world. The room seemed unbearably empty without them. He flung himself onto the bed and tried to tell himself that Arianwen was not gone forever. Surely he had the power to bring her back.

But he had nothing left for the wind. All Nain's gifts had been used up: the brooch, the whistle, the seaweed, and the scarf. Only one thing remained—the broken horse.

Gwyn got up and went over to the chest of drawers. He tried to open the top drawer but it seemed to be stuck. He shook it and the silver pipe rolled off the top. He bent to pick it up, and as he touched it, a sound came from it like whispering or the sea.

He ignored the sound and left the pipe on his bed while he continued to wrestle with the drawer. It suddenly burst open and almost fell out with the force that Gwyn had exerted on it.

The black horse lay within. It was alone and broken, grotesque without ears and a tail. Its lips were parted as if in pain, and Gwyn was overwhelmed by a feeling of pity. He took the horse out of the drawer and examined it closely. "*Dim hon!*" he murmured, reading again the tiny scrap of yellowing paper tied to its neck. "Not this! Why *Not this*? This is all I have!"

From the bed the pipe whispered, "Not this! Not this! Not this!"

But Gwyn was not listening.

The following morning Gwyn woke up with a sore throat and a cold.

"You'd better stay indoors," his mother told him over breakfast. "No use getting worse or spreading your germs."

Gwyn was about to remark that other people carried germs about, but thought better of it. He would not mind missing a day of school. And if, by some miracle, Arianwen had escaped the septic tank, she would fare better if she had a friend nearby.

"I'm not staying in bed!" he said sulkily. He had not forgiven his mother.

"I didn't say in bed," she retorted.

"I don't want to stay indoors either."

"Please yourself! I'm only thinking of your own good!"

Mr. Griffiths did not seem to be aware of the harsh tones flying round the breakfast table. He took himself off to the milking shed, still whistling.

Gwyn went up to the attic and put on his coat. The sun was shining and the air was warm. He went downstairs and out through the back door into the yard. To the left a row of barns formed a right angle with a long cowshed directly opposite the back door. To the right, a stone wall completed the enclosure. Within the wall a wide gate led to the mountain path. And somewhere in the field beyond that gate lay the septic tank.

Gwyn climbed over the gate and jumped down into the field.

A circle of hawthorn trees surrounded the area where the septic tank lay buried under half a meter of earth. The trees were ancient, their gray branches scarred with deep fissures. It always came as a surprise when white blossoms appeared on them in spring. Sheep had ambled round the thorn trees and nibbled the grass smooth. Not even a thistle was left to give shelter to a small stray creature.

Gwyn stood at the edge of the circle and contemplated the place where Arianwen may have ended her journey from the kitchen sink. He imagined her silver body whirling in a tide of black greasy water, and he was filled with helpless rage.

Thrusting his hands deep into his pockets, he stepped away from the hawthorn circle and began to stroll up the mountain. As the path wound upward, the field beside it sloped gently down towards the valley until, a mile beyond the farmhouse at a sharp bend, there was a sheer drop of ten meters from the path to the field below. Here, where a low stone wall gave some protection for the unwary, Gwyn stopped. There was something hard in his right pocket. He withdrew his hand and found that he was holding the broken horse. He must have slipped it into his pocket by accident the night before.

He stared at the poor broken thing and then looked back at the farmhouse. A wreath of smoke streamed from the chimney into the blue sky. A blackbird sang in the orchard, and he could see his mother hanging out the laundry. A breeze had set the pillowcases flying, and a pink curtain flapped from an upstairs window. It was such a peaceful, ordinary scene. And then his gaze fell upon the ring of hawthorn trees, and he hated the morning for being beautiful while Arianwen was dying in the dark.

Gwyn swung out his right hand and then hesitated. The horse seemed to be staring at him with its wild lidless eyes, inviting him to set it free. Its maimed mouth was grinning in anticipation. All at once Gwyn felt afraid of what he was about to do, but his grasp had slackened, and in that moment a gust of wind tore the horse away. His hand tightened on empty air. The wind carried the tiny object over a flock of sheep that neither saw nor cared about it. Some of the animals raised their heads when the boy above them cried out, "Go! Go then, and bring her back to me if you can! Arianwen! Arianwen! Arianwen!"

The broken horse vanished from sight, and as it did so, a low moan rumbled through the air. A black cloud passed across the sun, and the white sheep became gray.

Gwyn turned away to continue his walk, but after he had gone a few steps it began to rain—only a few drops at first, and then suddenly it was as if a cloud had burst and water poured down upon his head in torrents. He began to run back down the path. By the time he reached the house, the rain had become a hailstorm. His mother was bundling the wet laundry back into the kitchen, and Gwyn took an armful from her, fearing that it was he who had brought the storm upon them.

And storm it was, sudden, frightening, and ferocious. It beat upon the windows and tore into the barn roofs, causing the cattle to shift and grumble in their stalls. It shook the gates until they opened, and the terrified sheep poured into the garden and the yard. The hens shrieked and flapped battered, soaking wings as they ran to the hen house. And once there they added their voices to the terrible discord of the other animals.

The sky turned inky black, and Mrs. Griffiths put the lights on in the house. But the power failed and they were left in the dark, surrounded by the sounds of distressed creatures that they could not help.

Mr. Griffiths burst through the back door, his big boots shiny with mud.

"The lane's like a river," he exclaimed. "I've never seen anything like it."

"What is it, Ivor?" whispered his wife. "It was such a beautiful day."

"Just a storm." Mr. Griffiths tried to sound calm. "It'll blow itself out eventually."

Will it? Gwyn thought. Have I done this?

They lit a candle and sat round the table drinking tea. Mrs. Griffiths seemed the only one capable of speech. "Whatever's happened?" she kept murmuring. "It's like the end of the world. And Gwyn with a cold, too."

The storm abated a little in the afternoon. The hail turned to rain again, and they were able to attend to the animals. But the air still cracked and rumbled, and the dog was too terrified to work effectively. Gwyn and his father had a hard time driving the sheep out of the garden and through torrents of running mud to the field.

They managed to get the ewes into an open barn, where they remained, anxious but subdued.

"They'll lose their lambs if it goes on like this," said Mr. Griffiths.

The yard had become a whirlpool, and they had to use a flashlight to find their way safely to the cowsheds. The cows were in a state of panic. They trembled and twisted, bellowing mournfully. In the beam of light, the whites of their eyes bulged in their black faces. Though they were full of milk they refused to be touched.

Mr. Griffiths loved his black cows, loved to be close to them. He still milked by hand, ignoring the cold electric apparatus other farmers preferred. He stood in the cowshed suffering with his animals, dismayed by their condition.

"What is it?" he muttered. "It can't be the storm. I've never seen them like this."

"Leave them till later, Dad," Gwyn suggested. "They'll calm down when the wind dies."

"It's like the devil's in there," said his father, closing the big door on his cattle.

They waded back to the kitchen door, leaving their sodden raincoats and boots in the narrow porch outside. A cloud of water followed them into the room, but for once Mrs. Griffiths did not seem concerned. She was looking out of the window. "I'm thinking about Nain," she said. "The lane is like a river. Her front door rattles even in a breeze and you never fixed her roof in spring, like you said you would, Ivor."

"I'll go and see her in a bit." Her husband sighed and sank into a chair.

"I'll go," Gwyn offered. He wondered how Alun and the other Lloyds had fared in the storm.

The Lloyds were already at home. Fearing that her little ones would be soaked if they had to walk up the lane, Mrs. Lloyd had fetched her family by car. Just as well, for Iolo was wild with fear. He hated thunder.

Alun was in the room he shared with his brothers. He was standing by the window, watching the rain while the twins argued on the floor behind him. Alun enjoyed a storm. He relished the noise and the violence. He gazed at the contortions of the trees, hoping that one might fall. And then he saw something.

Someone was out in the storm, someone small and alone. A pale shape moving slowly against the wind and the water.

The figure stopped opposite the Lloyds' gate on the other side of the lane. Alun saw a white face looking up at him, and he knew who it was. Her hood had fallen back and her soaking hair hung in ash-colored strands over her hunched shoulders. She was holding one arm across her chest and looked frightened and exhausted.

Alun quickly drew the curtains and turned away from the window.

"What is it?" asked Gareth. "What did you see out there? You look funny."

"I didn't see nothing," Alun replied. "Only the storm."

"Looks like you saw a ghost to me," said Siôn.

Gwyn was on the front porch, putting on his boots. His mother helped him with his coat, buttoning it tightly at the neck.

"Don't be long, now," she said. "Just pop in and see if your grandmother needs anything. Come straight back or your cold'll get worse."

"It's gone," said Gwyn. "The water's washed it away." He tried to laugh, but the sound stuck in his throat.

He ran down the side of the path where the ground was higher, leaping from island to island, his flashlight aimed at the lane ahead.

When he reached his grandmother's cottage the rain suddenly stopped, and beneath the clouds an eerie yellow light crept across the horizon. The dripping trees stood black against the sky. The only sounds came from innumerable streams gushing down the mountainside.

There was no light in Nain's cottage. Gwyn knocked but there was no reply. He opened the door and looked in. His grandmother's room was cold and dark. There was something dreadfully wrong about the place, an oppressive stillness that frightened him. He turned on the light and saw what it was.

Beneath a gray veil of ashes, Nain's treasures lay in ruins. Pictures hung at crazy angles round the room, and once-bright scarves dropped in colorless shreds. The canary lay motionless at the bottom of its cage, and all about the floor were fragments of glass, books ripped and spoiled, shattered beads, and dying plants.

Some terrible element had crushed and abused everything in the room that was a part of his grandmother. Every object that she had chosen, nurtured, and loved had been destroyed.

Beside the dead fire, Nain sat huddled in a chair. She seemed older, smaller than before. There were ashes in her black hair and her face was gray.

Gwyn stepped slowly over the broken possessions until he stood beside his grandmother. "What has happened, Nain?" he asked. "What has been here?"

Nain looked up at him and her black eyes narrowed. "You know very well, Gwydion Gwyn," she said. "You know and I know what you have done. You crazy, bad magician!"

"What have I done, Nain?" Even as he asked the question, Gwyn knew what the answer would be.

"You let it go! My great-great-grandmother trusted me, and I trusted you. You have failed us, Gwydion Gwyn!"

"You mean the broken horse, don't you?" Gwyn cried defiantly. "Well, say so then! Speak its name! It was all I had! Arianwen has gone, drowned perhaps, and I had to get her back. Eirlys said I must!"

"But why the horse? Why the horse?" Nain rose out of her chair and her voice rose with her. "Didn't I tell you to keep it safe? Never to let it go? The spider would have returned to you. A creature like that could never die! She belongs to you, and you can get her when you want to, if you really try."

"I didn't know," said Gwyn. "And I didn't mean to let the horse go. The wind took it. What is it anyway, that I have released? And how can I stop it?"

"Only you can find that out, Gwydion Gwyn," his grandmother replied. "And I am afraid for you. It is a strong and dreadful thing that you must capture!"

"But didn't you see it? It was here. Why did it do this to your room?"

"Ah!" Nain sank back into her chair. "I tried to stop it, see. When I heard that noise in the air, and all the birds stopped singing . . . when the hail began to batter the land and the trees trembled, then I knew what you had done. So I went to my great-great-grandmother's books and I tried to find out how to stop it." Her voice sank to a whisper. "I burnt leaves in a bowl, and some bones and berries, and I began to sing. But it knew, didn't it? It knew what I was doing and it came in through the door and knocked me down. It smashed my bowl and blew out the fire, so angry it was. It roared round the room and broke everything in its way, and then it went!"

"And didn't you see *anything?*"

"Nothing! It was in the wind."

Gwyn was silent. He was terrified of the thing that he had to face. But he was determined to make reparation. "I'll help you clean up, Nain," he said.

"Leave it to me!" she snapped. "They'll be needing you at home."

But Gwyn refused to go until he had helped his grandmother sweep the debris from the floor. They gathered the dying plants and put them in water, then dusted the furniture, and straightened the pictures. Gwyn picked up the torn pages and replaced them in the books, and his grandmother tenderly arranged them into piles again. He sifted out the broken china and she put it in order, ready for glueing. After a while the room began to come to life. But the canary still lay quiet at the bottom of its cage, its neck bent and its eyes closed.

"It could do this?" Gwyn asked, staring at the broken bird.

"It could do worse," Nain replied. "Go on now! And take this." From beneath the cushion on which she had been sitting, she withdrew the black book. "I kept one thing safe, you see," she said. "I knew you would need it."

It was dark when he left the cottage. The water was not so deep and the thunder had rolled away, but there was a strange turbulence in the air that disturbed him.

He was relieved to see that the lights had come on

again in the farmhouse. It looked safe and welcoming. His father met him at the door. "Did you see the girl?" he asked.

Before Gwyn could reply, his mother said, "Why were you so long? What happened?"

"I had to help Nain," he explained. He would have said more if his father had not interrupted again.

"Did you see the girl?" he demanded anxiously.

"The girl? Eirlys? No, I didn't see her," Gwyn said.

"Where is she then?" His father sprang past him and strode across the lawn to where the Land Rover waited in its shed.

"The Herberts called," he shouted. "They said she left two hours ago. Slipped out of the house into the storm. Came to see if you were well, they thought, because you weren't at school!"

He disappeared into the shed and the Land Rover burst into life. It crashed down to the road and rocked and roared its way through the mud.

Two hours? Gwyn thought. And in the storm. Can she have fallen somewhere and I didn't see?

In the kitchen his mother had put four soup bowls on the table. "Your dad'll find her," she said when she saw Gwyn's worried frown.

Gwyn was not so sure. There was that thing in the air. That awful something that had destroyed Nain's room.

They heard the Land Rover returning only minutes later. Gwyn ran to open the front door. His father was already out of the vehicle. The door was swinging wide and he was gathering something into his arms, something gray, streaked with mud.

Mr. Griffiths walked through the gate and up the garden path. As he came within the arc of light from the porch, Gwyn and his mother saw the gray bundle more clearly. The girl's pale hair was black with mud, and her white face was covered with smudges of brown. She had lost her shoes.

Gwyn held his breath. He realized that he had known the girl for a long, long time. What a dull magician he was not to have understood, just because her hair was pale and her face white.

"I found her in the lane," said Mr. Griffiths, "just beside the Lloyds' wall. I can't imagine how they didn't see her. She's unconscious, from the cold probably. But I can't see any broken bones."

"I'll call Dr. Vaughan." Mrs. Griffiths ran to the telephone in the kitchen.

"She's staying here, Glenys," her husband called after her. "In Bethan's room. I'm not having them take her from us."

He carried the girl upstairs. Gwyn followed, mopping at the drops with a tissue. When Mrs. Griffiths had finished with the telephone, she ran up and covered the pillow with a towel. Then they gently removed the sodden gray coat and laid Eirlys on the bed.

They stood around the bed. Without saying a word, without even looking at each other, they knew that they had all seen this girl lying on the bright quilt before. They had seen her there long ago. They knew that Bethan had come back.

"You go and have your tea. I'll stay with her." Mr. Griffiths drew a chair up to the bed.

Gwyn did not move.

"Don't worry, lad," his father said. "It's all over now."

But Gwyn knew that it was not all over. Instead of eating, he took the flashlight down to the gate to watch for the doctor's car. Something black was lying beside the hedge, all huddled in the mud.

Gwyn bent down and picked up poor Long John's limp body. The black cat's eyes were closed, and his nose was full of earth. His three good legs had let him down at last, and he had drowned, unable to escape the malice of the storm.

"Who d'you think you are, you *thing*?" Gwyn screamed into the night. "I'll get you! Just you wait!"

8

THE TRAP

The doctor came late. He had many visits to make that night. Other mysterious accidents had occurred—falls, burns, and near-drownings.

When he had finished listening through his stethoscope, he held the girl's wrist for a long time, feeling her pulse. Something puzzled him. She reminded him of someone he had seen in the same house in that very room, only the other had been dark with golden skin. "It seems you have recovered," said Dr. Vaughan. "But you had better stay where you are for a day or two."

"Watch her," the doctor told Mrs. Griffiths before he went. "She's well, but her pulse is so weak I can hardly feel it. It's almost as though . . . no one were there."

Gwyn was allowed into the girl's room the following morning. It was still dark and the bedside light was

106

on. She was sitting up in one of Bethan's old night-dresses. Her hair had been washed and looked paler than ever.

It's strange she hasn't grown, thought Gwyn. Now we are the same size.

She was gazing round at all the things that made the room peculiarly Bethan's. A group of rag dolls on the dressing table in faded cotton dresses, a picture of blue-bells on the wall, a yellow dress in a plastic cover still hanging on the back of the door, and the blue and pink forget-me-not curtains that Bethan had chosen.

They did not refer to the past just then. They talked about the thing that had come hurtling out of the storm to throw her down into the mud, and about the terror of the animals, Nain's devastated rooms, and poor Long John.

"It's my fault," said Gwyn. "I know it is. I gave something to the wind that I should not have given. An old, old broken horse. I was told to keep it safe, never to let it go, but I wanted Arianwen back and I thought it was the only way."

"It seems to me," she said, "that if you are to stop the thing, you have to get its name, discover what it is."

"How can I do that?" Gwyn asked. "It could be one of a million names, like Rumpelstiltskin, and we can't wait that long. Who knows what damage it may do while we're searching for a name"

She rested her chin upon her hand, like Bethan used to do, and said slowly, "If you are your namesake, if

107

you are Gwydion, the magician from a legend, perhaps the broken horse is from a legend too. Perhaps a demon from a true story was trapped inside the broken horse by magic, to keep its evil locked up safe, away from the world."

Gwyn frowned. It seemed to make sense. It had felt so very old, that broken horse.

All at once the girl leaned forward and said quietly, "There was another gift, wasn't there? Nain gave you five. You have only told me about four of them!"

Gwyn looked hard at the girl in Bethan's bed. Then he said, "A yellow scarf. Your scarf, to bring you back!"

They grinned at each other. Gwyn felt as though all the heavy air that he'd been holding tight inside himself was flowing out of him and he could breathe again. He had so many questions to ask, he did not know which to choose. "Where have you been, Bethan?" he said at last.

"I'm not Bethan," she replied. "I might have been Bethan once, but now I'm Eirlys. I'll never be Bethan again. I've been out there!" She inclined her head, indicating a slither of darkness dividing the forget-me-not curtains.

"On the mountain?"

"No." She seemed reluctant to continue, and then said, "Out there! Further than the mountain! Further than the sky!"

"How?"

"It will be hard for you to believe."

"Go on. I know what it's like when people don't believe you. Tell me about the night you went to find the black ewe."

It was several minutes before Eirlys spoke again. Gwyn waited patiently while she searched for words to tell him what few people would believe.

"I wasn't frightened," she said slowly. "It was exciting out there with the rain shining in the flashlight. I had a feeling that something was going to happen. Something that I'd always wanted, but never understood. I couldn't find the black ewe. I called and called. You gave her a name, remember? Berry! Because her wool was purply black, like dark fruit. I had to go higher and higher, and it began to get cold. I'd forgotten my gloves and my fingers felt so stiff I could hardly hold the flashlight. I wanted to rest and warm my hands in my pockets, but I couldn't because of the light. And then I saw Berry. She was standing by that big rock, just past the last field, where it's quite flat. I called to her and I put out my hands—and I dropped the flashlight. It was so black. I tried to move in the dark, but I fell. I rolled and rolled, I don't know how far. Then I managed to grab a tuft of grass and stop myself."

The girl stopped speaking and stroked the patchwork quilt, spreading her fingers out as though she wanted to feel her way back to a place where she had once belonged.

"I thought I was going to die," she went on dreamily, "either from cold, or falling, or the wet. And then I saw a light, far away. There weren't any stars. The light came close and all around it the storm shone like a rainbow. I saw a sail and dancing creatures on a silver ship, just like you did. And I wanted to touch it. I wanted so much to be with it. . . ."

"And then?" Gwyn begged.

"They took me in!"

"Who took you in?"

"The children. Only they're not really children, they're quite old, and very wise. But they have never grown—like me. They took me to that other world. The place you saw in the web!"

"And Berry?"

"Berry was there too. She knew her name, but her fleece was silvery gray instead of black. And my hair was pale and so was my skin. And I never grew, nor did she."

"Is it a good place?"

"Yes, it is."

"Why did you come back?"

"You called me, didn't you? At first your calls were very faint, and then, when Nain gave you the gifts, your voice became so loud we couldn't ignore it. We sent the spider because you wanted to see me. She was all we had. That's how I could see you—in cobwebs!"

"Cobwebs?" said Gwyn. "You mean there are more

spiders? And you use them like . . . like television?"

Eirlys looked pityingly at him. "Not television," she said. "Our cobwebs are far more wonderful than that."

"Tell me more about the place out there. Could I go there?"

This time Eirlys ignored his question. "Find Arian-wen!" she said.

"But how? Mam drowned her. She's out there under the ground. I've nothing left, no gifts to get her back. And I don't know the words."

Eirlys stared at him. "You're a magician," she said. "You're Gwydion Gwyn. You can get her back. Try!"

Gwyn felt ashamed. Under the compelling gaze of those arctic eyes, he left the chair beside the bed and slipped silently out of the room.

He went downstairs and pulled on his boots. The rain had stopped and there was nothing to remind him that he would need a coat. He opened the front door, closing it noiselessly behind him. Within seconds he was standing outside the circle of hawthorn trees. There was something heavy in the air, forcing the gray, twisted branches to bend towards the earth, discouraging any passage beneath them.

Gwyn hesitated. Was it possible that even the trees were possessed? He stepped quickly into the circle and gasped as a thorn tore into his shoulder.

The sodden ground was beginning to freeze, and a white mist hung low over the grass. There was someone or something else within the circle. He could feel it, drawing him back towards the thorn trees. In order to resist it he had to fling himself to the ground and crawl towards the center.

Once there, Gwyn did not know what to do. He tried to remember how he had felt when he had hit Dewi Davis, but this was different. Something was distracting him, tugging his mind away from what he wanted to do. He lay his head on the freezing earth and listened, but all he could hear was the air above him, crackling like an angry firework. And then he too began to get angry. A deep hatred of the thing that had killed Long John boiled up inside him. He pushed and pushed against it with his mind until he felt it falling away and he had a clear space in his head.

He closed his eyes and thought of the bricks beneath the earth, the water from the kitchen sink within the bricks, the spider in the water. He brought up his hands to rest beside his head, thrust them downwards, and felt himself plunging through the earth. Down, down, down!

Mrs. Griffiths had come into the bedroom with a glass of milk. She gave the drink to Eirlys and then walked over to the window. "It's snowing again," she said. "What a start to the winter."

"I love the snow," said Eirlys.

"I know!" Mrs. Griffiths smiled. Then something through the window caught her eye. "Someone's out there," she said, "lying on the ground in the snow. Is it Gwyn?"

She opened the window to call to her son, but suddenly a shaft of lightning pierced the snow. With a deafening crack, it hit the ground just where Gwyn lay. Mrs. Griffiths screamed and fell to the floor. Eirlys, who had run to her, was the only one to see what happened within the circle of hawthorn trees.

She saw the ground sparkle and shake and Gwyn, arms outstretched, tossing like a bird in the wind. She saw his hands glowing in the snow, and the earth beneath them crack, and a shower of glittering icicles fly up and festoon the trees like tinsel. And in one of the trees something shone brighter than a star. She knew that Arianwen was safe.

Only then did Eirlys run to fetch a cold washcloth. She laid it on Mrs. Griffiths' head and gently stroked her hair.

Mrs. Griffiths opened her eyes. "It's you," she said, taking the girl's hand. "What happened? I felt queer, and so afraid."

"It's the snow," Eirlys replied. "It's the whiteness. It makes you feel queer sometimes."

Mrs. Griffiths sat up, still keeping the girl's hand clasped in hers. "It's so good to have you here," she said.

They stayed quite still for a moment, the girl kneeling beside the woman, calm and silent, until Mrs. Griffiths suddenly got to her feet exclaiming, "What a nurse I am. It's you who's supposed to be the patient. Back to bed now or the doctor will be telling me off!"

She had just tucked the girl's blankets in again when Gwyn appeared in the doorway. He was wet with snow and smiling triumphantly.

"Gwyn! Was that you out there?" his mother asked. "Lying in the snow? Are you mad?"

"No, not mad—a magician!" he replied.

Mrs. Griffiths made a clicking noise with her tongue. "I don't know," she said. "Sometimes I wonder if Mrs. Davis wasn't right about you."

"Can I talk to Eirlys for a bit?"

"You ought to be in school," his mother said, "but seeing as you aren't, yes, you can have a chat. Change your clothes first, and dry your hair!"

Gwyn retreated. When he returned, dry, to the bedroom, he was carrying his grandmother's black book. "I've got Arianwen," he said. He held out his hand, allowing the silver spider to crawl onto the patchwork quilt. "I had to fight for her. Something was trying to stop me."

"I saw," said Eirlys. "You *are* a magician, Gwyn!"

Gwyn was gratified, yet a little embarrassed. "I've been looking at Nain's book," he told the girl, "and I can read it. I never thought I could."

"Read it to me then, and we'll try and find the demon in the broken horse!"

Gwyn sat on the bed and began to read the old

Welsh legends, translating as he went. It was not an easy task, but the more he read, the more fluent he became. Eirlys heard again the stories that she half remembered from the time when Nain had sat where Gwyn was sitting now, talking on and on until she slept.

She heard about kings and princes, magicians and giants, and even the knights of King Arthur. But nowhere could Gwyn find a broken horse.

"Read about Princess Branwen," Eirlys said. "There are horses in that legend, I remember. It used to make me cry, but I've forgotten it."

Gwyn began the story of Branwen. He had read almost two pages when he suddenly stopped and said quietly, "I have found it. But it is too terrible to read aloud. I can't read it!"

"Tell me," said Eirlys.

"I can't!" Gwyn stared at the page. There were tears in his eyes.

"Tell me!" she insisted.

"You'll hate it," said Gwyn. And then he read, " 'Efnisien, Branwen's brother, came upon the King of Ireland's horses. "Whose horses are these?" he asked. "They belong to the King of Ireland," said the soldiers. "He has come to marry your sister, Branwen." And Efnisien screamed, "No one asked me. No one asked my consent. She shall not marry the King of Ireland!" He drew his sword, and, filled with rage and hatred, he cut off the horses' ears and their tails, their eyelids and their lips, until they screamed with pain, and no one could touch them!' "

Silence filled the room. "You're sorry now, I told you!" Gwyn said.

"No!" Eirlys had drawn the quilt around her neck. "We had to know. Perhaps that mad prince never died, but became locked in the broken horse because of what he'd done!"

"Nain tried to burn the horse, but she couldn't," said Gwyn.

"It couldn't be destroyed so it was given to the magicians to keep safe," Eirlys suggested. "They were the most powerful men in the land in those days!" She paused and then said, "Well, you know whom you have to catch!"

"I know his name, but I can't see him. How do I know where he is?"

"He's on the mountain, for sure. You'll be able to feel him. And you have Arianwen to help you!"

Gwyn went to the window and drew the curtains wide. It was light now and snowflakes were flying past the window. Some would linger in their journey and dance gently up and down against the pane before drifting on to the apple tree below.

"Perhaps you'd better wait," said Eirlys, when she saw the snow. "There'll be a blizzard on the mountain."

"No! I don't dare wait. Something will happen if I don't stop him now. I won't go far. I know what to do. Tell Mam I've gone to see Nain."

Mrs. Griffiths was in the kitchen when Gwyn slipped downstairs, put on his coat and boots, and, for the second time that morning, crept out of the house.

He realized as soon as he was through the door that he would not get far. Eirlys was right. There was a blizzard on the mountain. The wind and snow lashed his face, and he had to screw up his eyes and look down at his boots in order to make any headway. But he knew the way, and he knew what he had to do.

When he arrived at the stone wall where he had flung the broken horse, he took Arianwen from his pocket and held her out to the snow. She clung to his hand for a moment, bracing herself against the wind.

"Go!" Gwyn whispered. And then words came to him that he had never known and did not understand, and he began to chant.

The spider rolled off Gwyn's hand and drifted up into the snow. He watched her, shining silver amongst the white flakes, and then he had to shut his eyes against the blizzard. When he opened them the spider was gone, and already the wind had slackened.

There was a sudden stillness as the mountain held its breath. Clouds of snow began to gather on the summit. They intensified and rolled downwards in a vast, ever-thickening ice-cold wave. In a few seconds Gwyn could hardly see his hands. He felt for the stone wall and found instead something smooth and tall—a pillar of ice!

And then Gwyn ran, or rather threw himself, snow-blind and stumbling, down the path and away from his spell. Arianwen had begun to spin!

At that moment, someone was knocking on the farmhouse door. Mrs. Griffiths opened it and found Alun Lloyd on the doorstep.

"It is Alun, isn't it?" she asked, for the boy was muffled up to his eyes in a thick red scarf.

"Yes," Alun mumbled through the scarf.

"You've not gone to school, then?"

"No school." The reply was just audible. "No bus—blizzard—where's Gwyn?"

"Stamp the snow off those boots and come in!" said Mrs. Griffiths. She took the boy's coat and shook it outside before closing the door. "Gwyn's upstairs with the girl," she went on. "Poor little thing had an accident yesterday. She's in bed!"

"I heard," muttered Alun. "Can I go up?"

" 'Course, love. First door on the left. Don't stay too long, mind. She's still a bit—"

Alun had sprung up the stairs before Mrs. Griffiths could finish her sentence. He opened the door and saw only the girl. She was sitting up in bed, reading a book.

"Where's Gwyn?" Alun asked.

"With his grandmother," the girl replied.

"No, he's not. I've been there!"

The two children stared at each other across the patterned quilt.

Alun decided to put his question another way. "Is he in the house? Won't he see me?"

The girl regarded him gravely, and he had to look away from her strange, greeny blue gaze. He did not like her eyes. They made him feel cold.

"O.K. You're not going to tell, are you? I'm sorry about . . . about your falling down and that, and I came to say so." He glanced briefly at her pale face, then quickly averted his eyes again. "But I want to tell Gwyn about it. I want to talk to him, see? And I'm going to find him. I don't care if it takes—forever!"

Alun turned swiftly and ran out of the room.

A few seconds later Mrs. Griffiths heard the front door slam and called out, "Was that Alun? Why didn't he stay?" Receiving no reply, she returned to her washing, still unaware that Gwyn was not in the house.

Outside, Alun saw footsteps in the snow and began to follow them.

Gwyn returned minutes later. He took off his snow-soaked coat and boots and crept barefoot up to the bedroom.

"It's done!" he told Eirlys. "The spell's begun!"

"Your friend was here!" she said.

"Alun? What did he want?"

"To see you! He was angry!"

"Where has he gone?" Gwyn felt a terrible apprehension take hold of him.

"I think he went on to the mountain," Eirlys replied with equal consternation.

"I didn't see him. He must have missed the path!"

"He'll get lost!"

"Trapped!" cried Gwyn. "Trapped and frozen!" He tore down the stairs and out into the snow, in his panic forgetting to put on his boots or his coat or to shut the front door. As he ran he called his friend's name again and again, until he was hoarse. The snow had become a fog, still and heavy, like a blanket, smothering any sound.

He found his way to the place where he had touched the pillar of ice. There was another beside it now, and another and another. They rose higher than he could reach and were too close to pass through. A wall of ice! Gwyn beat upon the wall, kicked it, and tore at it with his fingers, all the while calling Alun's name in his feeble croaking voice. And then he slid to the ground, defeated by his own spell.

9

RETURN

Gwyn's mother was waiting for him when he stumbled home. "You left the door open," she accused him. "Whatever have you been doing? Where's Alun?"

Gwyn could not tell her. The trap had been set and now there was nothing anyone could do until Arianwen had finished her work. Besides, Alun might have gone home. They had no proof that he was on the mountain. "I think he's gone home," Gwyn told his mother.

But later that day, when Mr. Lloyd arrived searching for his eldest son, Gwyn admitted, "Yes! Alun was here," and "Yes! He might have gone up on the mountain. But I didn't know. I didn't know for sure!"

Then Mrs. Lloyd, who had followed her husband with little Iolo, turned on Gwyn and vented all her anger and fear. "He was your friend," she cried. "He came to look for you! Why didn't you go after him? Why didn't you say? Don't you remember how it was when your sister went? It's been four hours now! Don't you care? Don't you care about anyone, Gwyn Griffiths? You're not normal, you aren't! Not a normal boy at all!"

Little Iolo began to scream, and Gwyn's fingers ached with the desire to hurt. But he could not use his power, because he knew this woman was terribly afraid. How could she know that he was suffering as much as she? He left the kitchen and went up to his room.

The fog was so dense he could see nothing out of his window. He knew he had to protect Alun, but how? And then he remembered something Nain had said about those long-ago magicians. "They could turn men into eagles!" Why could he not turn Alun into a bird —a small bird—a white one, so that he could not be seen against the snow?

He scanned the room for something that had belonged to Alun. On his bookshelf was an old paperback book on boats that Alun had lent him. It hardly seemed appropriate, but it would have to do. He took the book to the window and held it very tight. He closed his eyes and tried to picture Alun, tried to remember every feature of his friend: his blue eyes, his freckles, his short red fingers with the nails all bitten. And then he thought of a bird, a small white bird, and he placed the picture of the bird that was in his mind over the blue eyes, the freckled nose, and the tufty fair hair of his friend, until the bird and the boy seemed to become one.

Gwyn did not know how long he stood by the window. He was not aware of any sound until the search party began to arrive. The grapevine in Pendewi worked fast. Sometimes people even sensed the news before they heard it. Ten men set off to look for Alun Lloyd, and later Mrs. Griffiths and another mother followed them.

The search did not last long. Gwyn heard the defeated stamping of boots in the snow, the grave, deep voices, and the kettle whistling on and on and on!

Hunger and curiosity drove him downstairs. The kitchen was so crowded he could not find a chair, nor reach the bread bin. He managed to sneak a plate of cookies from the table, and then retreated with it to the door. He leaned and listened, waiting for someone to mention the mountain and whatever it was that Arianwen had built there.

They were all talking at once, yet avoiding what they wanted to say. They were adults and did not know how to discuss something that was impossible, something they did not understand.

Pools of water on the kitchen floor mingled with crushed cookies and cigarette ash. Iolo was under the table, snivelling, but everyone had become accustomed to that sound and ignored him. Gwyn remembered that other search, four years ago, when he had sat under the table and cried because his sister was lost.

And then the words that he wanted to hear began to drift towards him.

"Did you feel it?" "Bloody peculiar!" "Like a net!" "A cloud?" "No, not that!" "Ice!" "A frozen cloud?" "More like a wall!" "Never heard of anything like it!" "Call the police!" "What can they do?" "Can't see a bloody thing out there!" "Searchlights?"

Gwyn sidled out the door and carried his plate of cookies upstairs. He heard the police arrive. Eirlys, the last person to see Alun, was called down to speak to them.

Everybody stopped talking when she came in. They drew back and gazed at the frail, white-faced child, so insubstantial and fairylike in her white nightgown and borrowed gray shawl. She brought to mind that other time, in the same farmhouse, when they had come to search for a girl like this one, so very like this one. Only the other girl had been dark and rosy-cheeked, and they had never found her. Now they bent their heads, straining to hear the words she spoke so softly. And when she had finished, they all began to sigh and murmur about mists and mountains. Officer Perkins had to erase half his notes. He was new to the area, just up from the city, and he felt like a stranger among these superstitious and excitable farmers. Their melodious voices conveyed nothing but confusion to him.

He left with his partner, Officer Price, and they walked up the road for a bit, to find out what they could. They returned before long, and drove away without a word.

It'll be in the papers, thought Gwyn. They'll call it a phenomenon and then they'll forget about it.

The searchers departed in ones and twos. "We'll be back in the morning!" they called. "We'll find him!"

The Lloyds were the last to leave. Iolo had fallen asleep in his father's arms, but now Mrs. Lloyd was crying.

It was such a long, long night. Gwyn could not sleep. He sat on the edge of his bed and stared at the window. Eirlys came up and kept him company. They did not speak, but her presence was comforting. Just as she was about to go, a sound came from the mountain. A long, wailing sigh!

"Did you hear that?" Gwyn whispered.

"Was it the wind?" she asked.

"No, not the wind!"

The sound came again, louder this time. An anguished, melancholy howl. It crept down Gwyn's spine and made him shiver.

"It's like a wild animal," said Eirlys.

"Trapped!" he added.

The howling gradually died away, and Eirlys returned to her bed. But later that night it came again, louder and more terrible than ever, though it seemed to be only Gwyn who heard it. It got into his head, and he had to rock back and forth to endure the sound. He knew who it was, of course, and agonized over what it might do to Alun, if it found him.

And then he became aware that the sound was in the room. It was in the silver pipe, lying on the bedside table.

Gwyn jumped out of bed, seized the pipe, and ran with it across the room. He thrust it into his drawer and slammed the drawer tightly shut. But to his horror, the voice within the drawer merely seemed to intensify, until the whole chest vibrated with the sound.

Gwyn put his hands over his ears and stumbled backwards to the bed. He knows about the pipe, Gwyn thought. He's using it to fight me. But he won't get out! He won't! He won't! Arianwen and I are too strong for him!

It ended at last. Gwyn lay back, exhausted, and fell asleep on top of the blankets.

He was awakened by another sound, a muffled, intermittent tapping on his window. Someone was throwing snowballs.

He went to the window, opened it, and looked out. A shadowy figure was beside the apple tree, but he could not make out any features. "Who's there?" he called.

"Alun!" came the reply.

Gwyn ran down and opened the front door.

Alun was standing on the porch. He was pale, but certainly not frozen. He was holding something small and dark in his hand, and he had an odd, vacant expression in his eyes, as though he was not sure why or how he had come to be there. He stepped into the house and wordlessly followed Gwyn into the kitchen. He laid the thing that he had been holding on the kitchen table. It was the broken horse!

Gwyn stared at it. "Where've you been?" he asked gently.

"Out there!" Alun jerked his head towards the window.

"I know, out there," said Gwyn. "But where?"

Alun wiped his nose on the sleeve of his coat. He did not seem inclined to answer any more questions.

"Better take some of that off," said Gwyn, nodding at his friend's soaking clothes.

Alun removed his coat, his boots, and his socks, and then he sank onto a kitchen chair and wiped his nose, this time on his shirt cuff.

"Wish you could tell me about it!" Gwyn bit his lip. He realized that it was no use trying to force Alun to talk. He would have to wait until his friend was ready.

"Aw heck!" Alun scratched his head. "I don't know. It's all so peculiar, like. I don't really understand what happened. I was following your footsteps in that blizzard, and I got lost. So I turned around to come back

—and I couldn't. There was something there, like bars. Ice-cold they were, but hard as anything. At first it was all cloudy, and I couldn't see, but then it got brighter and brighter and I saw what I was caught in. It was a sort of cage, bars all round in a pattern, like a . . . like a . . ."

"Cobweb?" Gwyn suggested.

"Phew!" Alun looked hard at Gwyn. "You know, don't you? It's funny though. All those things you said. They were true, weren't they?"

"Yes, they were true!"

"Well, I suppose you know about the man, then?"

"What man?" Gwyn stepped closer. "Was there a man in there with you?"

"A kind of man. He scared me. He had red hair and he was dressed all in kind of bright stuff, jewelry and that, with a cloak and a gold belt with a big sword in it. And he was beating at the bars with his fists, tearing at them, banging his head on them, yelling. I was scared, I can tell you. But he didn't see me. It sounds funny, but I felt very small and kind of . . . like I had something round me, very warm and soft, like feathers. Anyway, he kept on and on at those bars for hours and hours. I fell asleep, and when I woke up he was still at it—moaning and crying. And then something awful happened!"

Gwyn waited. He could hardly bear the suspense, but he dared not ask a question.

"He began to disappear," Alun continued, "just

shrank. Sort of faded away, and so did the bars of ice, until there was nothing left there, except . . ."

"Except what?"

"That!" Alun pointed to the broken horse.

Gwyn looked at it, lying on its side, black and disfigured. Poor thing! he thought. You want so much to get out—but I can never, never let you. He took the horse and slipped it into his pocket. Later he would find a safe and secret place.

It was all over, and suddenly he felt very tired.

There were sounds from above, and Gwyn said, "They've been looking for you, your dad and mine."

"I bet!" said Alun.

"And Mr. Davis came, and Gary Pritchard's dad, and Mr. Ellis and Mr. Jones, Tŷ Gwyn, and people I can't remember. Even Mrs. Pritchard came, and she and my mam went out to look. And your mam was here with Iolo. I don't know why she brought him, he was making such a racket."

"He always does." Alun nodded sympathetically.

Mrs. Griffiths came into the kitchen and gasped at the sight of Alun sitting there so rosy and cheerful. Before she could utter a word the doorbell rang. The Lloyds had returned to resume their search.

Mrs. Griffiths ran to open the door. "He's back!" she cried. "He's safe, your Alun. Good as new and nothing wrong with him, as far as I can see."

"Where? Where?" Mrs. Lloyd tore into the kitchen and flung herself upon her son.

"Come on, Mam. I'm O.K.," came Alun's muffled voice from beneath his mother.

"What happened? Where've you been? They went to search. We thought you'd freeze!"

"I stayed where I was," Alun said, wriggling. "I didn't want to get lost. I got behind some rocks . . . in a sort of cave. It was quite warm, really."

Mrs. Lloyd began to wrap up her boy like a baby, though the mist had gone and the sky was brightening. She bundled him out into the hallway, talking nonstop to her husband and Mrs. Griffiths. While she spoke, Alun looked back at Gwyn and said, "I found this out there, as well." He put something cool into Gwyn's hand—the snow spider.

Gwyn curled his fingers round the spider as Alun whispered hoarsely, "Don't tell about . . . about what I said, will you?"

"I won't tell!" Gwyn grinned. "One loony's enough!"

Alun grinned back and gave the thumbs-up sign. And then his mother whisked him through the door.

Mr. Griffiths had his way, and Eirlys stayed for Christmas. It was the sort of Christmas one always remembers. The trees were iced with snow and the sun came out to make the mountain sparkle. The biggest Christmas tree they had ever seen at Tŷ Bryn was put up in the front room and decorated with lights like candles, silver stars, and homemade sweets wrapped in colored paper.

A log fire was lit, and they all played Monopoly and Scrabble, and even made up games so as to prolong the fun. Mrs. Griffiths played carols on the out-of-tune piano with damp hammers, and it did not matter that the soloists were sometimes out of tune, too. The children were allowed to drink punch, which made them giggle at Nain, who had drunk too much and looked like a Christmas tree herself, all bedecked in colored beads and bangles.

Just before they went to bed, Eirlys looked out of the window at the white, moonlit mountain and said, "It reminds me of home!" Only Gwyn heard her. He knew that she was not talking about Wales, and it occurred to him for the first time that she might not stay with them forever.

On New Year's Day, the children decided to walk in the fields. It was a cold day, and while the girl waited in the garden, Gwyn ran up to fetch the gloves his father had given him for Christmas. They were blue and silver, lined with fur, and Gwyn cherished them even more than the black watch his mother had given him for his birthday.

When he opened his drawer he saw Arianwen and the silver pipe. They looked so innocent, who would guess what they could do? One that had travelled a million miles or more, the other from somewhere in the distant past. They would always be with him now, he knew that. As he turned away, the pipe whispered something. It sounded like, "Don't go!" Gwyn smiled and drew on his gloves. "I'm not going anywhere!" he said.

His parents were outside in the garden with Eirlys. They were standing by the gate, talking quietly while they stared up at the mountain. They did not see Gwyn when he came out, nor hear him close the front door.

"I have to go soon," Eirlys was saying. "I have to go back to where I came from."

His parents did not speak immediately. They seemed frozen by her remark. Then Mrs. Griffiths put her hand out and gently tucked the girl's hair into her hood. "Do you have to go, Eirlys? Can't you stay?"

Eirlys shook her head.

"Were you happy there, where you came from?" Mr. Griffiths asked.

"Oh, yes! Very happy!"

They did not ask where she lived. They did not seem to want to know. And then Gwyn broke into their thoughts. "Come on," he cried, "I'll race you to the trees!" He ran past them through the open gate.

Eirlys followed, and they ran to the circle of hawthorn trees where Gwyn had released Arianwen. The snow had melted and the grass was smooth and green. There was nothing to show that the earth had shaken or that icicles had flown from it like stars.

"Why couldn't she escape without my help?" Gwyn thought aloud. "She has her own power."

"She has nothing without you," said Eirlys. "She needs your thoughts to help her."

"She's just an ordinary spider, then?"

"Oh, no! No creature from my place is a common garden thing!"

My place! There it was again. "Are you leaving here?" He put the question cautiously.

"Today!" she answered.

"What? So soon? You can't!"

"They are coming for me!" she looked up at the sky. "Even with your magic I only had until today."

"Do you want to go?"

"Oooooh, yes!" Her reply came like a deep contented sigh.

"But Mam and Dad?"

"They understand. I said I had to go back to where I came from."

Gwyn nodded. "They wouldn't want to know the truth," he said.

"I think they do know. But they're too old now to be able to talk about it."

"And they don't mind you going?"

She shook her head and smiled at him. "It'll be all right now between you and Dad. He knows I'm safe. That's all he wanted."

"And the Herberts?"

"I'm just a number that got muddled up. They think I've gone already."

They had begun to walk up the path without his really being aware of it. When they had passed the first bend and the farm had disappeared from sight, Gwyn suddenly stopped to look at a kestrel hanging motionless in the air. Cloud shadows raced across the snow-capped mountains beyond the bird, and a truck piled with golden hay made its way slowly across the green fields below.

"Won't you miss all this?" Gwyn asked.

"No!" she said. "I like it where I'm going."

He noticed the cold first, before he saw anything. "I don't think I'll come any further," he said.

"Come on! Just for a bit, to keep me company!" She took his hand.

Her fingers seemed colder than ever, but he allowed himself to be led away from the path and through the fields of sheep. And then he saw the light, glinting now and then through the billows of a great, gray cloud. He felt an icy breeze on his face.

"You go on," he said. "I'm staying here!" He tried to pull his hand away, but she would not let him. They were approaching the flat field where Bethan had gone to rescue the black ewe, four years before.

"Let me go!" cried Gwyn.

Her fingers tightened on his wrist. He twisted and turned, but her grip was like steel, her strength irresistible. He could see the ship now, falling slowly through the clouds, the great sail swelling, the dancing creatures sparkling on the hull. Icy fragments spun earthwards, and terrified sheep swung away from the field and scattered in a great wave past the children.

"Let me go!" Gwyn begged.

"Come with me!" Her soft voice floated above the moan of the wind, "Come!"

"No!" Gwyn screamed. "I want to stay. No! No! No! Leave me!"

"Come!" She looked back at him and smiled, but her fingers bit deeper into his wrist. "Please!" she sighed. "I need you, Gwyn. We need you—out there!"

"No!" Gwyn began to shake, and through his tears he saw the ship as a huge, glittering cloud behind the girl's pale shape. Then a voice inside him suddenly burst out, "Gwydion lives *here!*" and he pulled free from her grasp and flung himself to the ground.

He lay there with his eyes closed, nursing his aching hand. When the bitter cold and all the threatening sounds had vanished, he got up and saw something where Eirlys had been—the yellow scarf, frozen into the snow, and the seaweed beside it. He picked them up. He put the seaweed into his pocket, but the scarf was stiff with frost, like a strange, twisted stick.

He wandered slowly through the fields until he came to the path. There, on the last bend, he found Alun standing by the stone wall.

"What's that?" Alun asked.

"Someone's scarf," said Gwyn. "Look, it's still frozen!"

"Where's the girl?"

"She's gone!"

"Phew!" said Alun.

They walked back to the farm in comfortable silence. Mr. Griffiths was standing on the porch when they arrived, "She's gone, then?" he said.

"Yes!" Gwyn replied. And then, before his father could turn away, he said, "I'm not going, Dad. I'm not ever going!"

"I know!" Mr. Griffiths smiled. "And I'm glad of that, Gwyn! Very glad!"

They went into the house. A house that was not empty anymore.